Matt —
Enjoy the book.

Outdoor Follies

Peter F. Crowley

Published by:
B&J Press, LLC
65464 Lake Park Road,
Ashland, Wisconsin 54806

Original Copyright 2004 © by Peter F. Crowley
Illustrations 2006 B&J Press, LLC
First Edition 2007
Printed in the United States

All inquires should be addressed to:
B&J Press, LLC
65464 Lake Park Road
Ashland, WI 54806

ISBN-13: 978-0-9791635-0-0
ISBN-10: 0-9791635-0-1

All rights reserved. No part of this book may be reproduced, stored in a retrieval system, or transmitted in any form or by any means, electronic, mechanical, photocopying, recording, or otherwise, without written permission of the publisher. For information regarding permission, write to Permission Dept., B&J Press. LLC.

Library of Congress Control Number: 2006911126

Illustration by Karen & Bill Maki

DEDICATION

••••••••••••••••

For Bob and Julie.

ACKNOWLEDGEMENTS

•••••••••••••••••••••••••••••

Many people helped me make this book a reality. They include Abby Knoblauch, for her insight into the world of publishing; Gyneth Slygh, PhD, for her expert opinion; Dan Small, PhD, Outdoor Wisconsin Television, for his encouragement, editorial opinion and willingness to take time from his extremely busy schedule to help me; Karen and Bill Maki, for the front cover art; and especially Bill Maki, for his many hours of editorial help. Without the help of these people, this book would never have been published.

I would like to sincerely thank all these people.

Peter F. Crowley

FOREWORD

∙∙∙∙∙∙∙∙∙∙∙∙

Pete Crowley is an incredibly lucky man. Over a span of more than 50 years, he has braved thin ice, intense storms and treacherous swamps in search of adventure in Wisconsin's North Woods and has somehow managed to survive one serious mishap after another. He has broken through the ice miles offshore on Lake Superior, fallen head-first from the top of a spruce tree and nearly drowned while trying to climb back into his still-moving boat after it threw him overboard at full throttle.

As you might have guessed, Crowley himself was the cause of most of these mishaps. He not only survived them, he turned them into a howling collection of stories, some of them frighteningly true, some outrageously fabricated. The mishaps he recounts in the few stories that purport to be factual suggest there has been no shortage of such events to draw from as he crafted those that stretch the truth.

Crowley spins a good yarn, and he has a knack for dragging the reader along, as one unlikely event follows another on the way to an almost-believable outcome. Through them all, Crowley portrays himself as a stalwart woodsman, cunning hunter of everything from mice to bears, and bumbling fall guy for whom just about everything that can go wrong, does. If Murphy hadn't already claimed that law, Crowley certainly could have.

If you have ever stayed one cast too long on the water, slogged one mile too far up the trail or thrown one too many logs on

FOREWORD CONTINUED

the fire, then it's a safe bet you'll find yourself in some of Crowley's misadventures. They offer us many lessons, the greatest of which might be that sometimes the best we can hope for is a good laugh.

Dan Small
PhD, Producer, *Outdoor Wisconsin Television*

CONTENTS

∙∙∙∙∙∙∙∙∙∙∙

The Fish Stretcher	*1*
The Great Bay City Creek Canoe Run	*13*
The Education of a Turkey Hunter	*21*
A Memorable Duck Hunt	*37*
How I Earned an "A" in Senior English	*45*
My Three Lives	*55*
Bear Grease	*67*
Camp Pranks	*73*
Adventures with Food	*83*
A Memorable Turkey Hunt	*91*
Survival While Ice Fishing Manual	*99*
Big Hill	*107*
Camp Orienta	*117*
Bearing Up Under Father	*129*
The Two Hundred Dollar Fish Fry	*137*
Uncle Tom	*149*
Why I Never Became a Big Game Guide	*159*
Camp Mice	*165*

PREFACE

This book is a collection of mostly humorous outdoor stories. There are three serious stories: My Three Lives, A Memorable Duck Hunt and A Memorable Turkey Hunt. Those stories are true. The other stories are humorous and although based on actual events, I took the liberty of changing names, times, events and characters so they would be unrecognizable to the actual participants. Well, almost unrecognizable.

If you're like most people, you'll find yourself somewhere in these stories. Reading them will transport you back to a time and place in your past when you experienced the joy, adventure and freedom of the outdoors.

Peter F. Crowley

THE FISH STRETCHER

∙∙∙∙∙∙∙∙∙∙∙∙∙∙∙∙∙∙∙∙∙∙∙∙∙∙

They are an evil fish. Oh sure, they're good eating and good fighters but those traits have only evolved to better sucker fishermen into chasing them. I believe this species has a plan to rid Lake Superior of what they consider a great evil . . . fishermen. How? By purposely luring fishermen onto thin ice, hoping they'll fall through.

I also think these fish may have learned that the legal limit is fifteen inches and are evolving into a strain that stops growing lengthwise at fourteen and nine-tenths inches. I'm not certain about this; it could be that the Department of Natural Resources (DNR) is also involved. The DNR plant most of these fish and they may have altered their genetics in such a way that these fish stop growing lengthwise at fourteen and nine-tenths inches. Why? So the DNR can reap huge piles of money from fining fishermen caught with undersized fish.

What fish can this be, you ask? This diabolical fish is a splake.

Lake trout and brook trout are native to Lake Superior. They are both from the char family and occasionally the milt of one of these species fertilizes the eggs of the other. The eggs hatch and produce a fish called a splake. Splake are beautiful fish and have some of the characteristics of both lake trout and brook trout. Unfortunately, at least as far as the splake are concerned, they are also a hybrid and except in rare cases, are unable to reproduce. This makes them very angry and may account for their devilish behavior.

There are a lot of lake trout in Lake Superior but very few brook trout, consequently there are very few native splake. It may have been better to allow this unhappy species to dwindle to near extinction but the DNR had other ideas. They decided that the Lake should be full of these fish and have been planting substantial numbers of hatchery-raised splake fingerlings.

People who have never fished for splake think that because splake are good eating, good fighters and easy to catch, they're the perfect fish. I disagree!

Why? In the summer, when they could be fished from the safety of a boat, they disappear. Nobody knows where they go. Therefore, if you want to fish for splake, you're forced to fish for them through the ice. What's more, these clever creatures will not remain under stable ice! They constantly move toward thin ice. Some people, like those silly fish biologists for example, say that's because there's more oxygen under thin ice. I say it's because they're trying to lure the fishermen out until they fall through the ice. Then there's the size issue. Nine out of ten splake caught measure fourteen and nine-tenths inches, just small enough to be illegal. Once they reach fourteen and nine-tenths inches in length, they start growing deeper and wider. Either it's a result of a previously unheard of evolutionary spurt or they are being genetically altered by the DNR.

Because Lake Superior is so vast, it doesn't freeze all at once. Ice forms near the shore first and then slowly forms farther out. Therefore, the farther out you go, the greater the risk. The splake have learned this.

To keep you interested, they bite well when the ice initially forms. Then, when they've got you hooked, the fishing slows down and you're forced to go farther out to find them again. And once you've caught a few, the temptation to chase after them is overwhelming. I'm certain that splake do this on purpose. They're constantly moving farther and farther out, until splash! Another fisherman falls in the drink, spills his minnows and the splake show up for a free lunch.

This year I had a plan to defeat them. The two major problems were short fish and thin ice. During the summer I came up with a solution to both problems. The thin ice problem was easy. I bought the largest plastic sled I could find. It looked like a pram. Heck, it practically was a pram. I tested it in the shallow water near shore and although it floated a little low in the water, I was able to get in and paddle around. The second problem was a little more difficult but I finally came up with a solution. I called it a "fish stretcher." I built a wooden box that was open on the top and had a wire affixed to one end. It worked by laying the fish in the box, looping the wire around its tail and securing it to one end. Then another wire is looped around the gills and attached to a little toy winch that was fixed to the other end of the box. It would only take a short stretch to make up the one-tenth of an inch difference, surely not a crime. I didn't bother to try it out beforehand because I was too busy trying to get my antler stretcher finished before deer season.

The ice formed on Lake Superior's Chequamegon Bay on December fourteenth. Two days later a few guys were tentatively creeping out from shore in search of splake. I decided to give it a try.

I called my fishing partner, Jerry, and asked him if he wanted to go splake fishing the next day. "Yeah, I suppose," he said, "how thick is the ice?"

"There's plenty of ice," I answered. "I'll pick you up at 8:00 a.m."

The next morning while Jerry was loading his gear in my truck, he asked, "What did you say we're going to fish for?"

"Splake," I answered.

"Just a minute, Pete, I gotta go back in the house."

"Why?"

"Because I want to get a life jacket, bring my will up to date, show Donna where the life policies are and kiss the dog goodbye."

"Don't worry," I said, "we'll be careful. I'll guarantee you we won't take any chances. Anyway, I got a plan."

"That's what you said when you swamped the boat last duck season!"

"That was an unavoidable accident," I said. "It was dark. Anyway, it was your fault, you should have reminded me to put the plug in the boat. Now, where's your snowmobile and trailer so we can hook it up?"

"My snowmobile? Forget it! Why don't we use yours?"

"You can't be serious, Jerry. Use my brand new eight thousand dollar touring sled? I've only got two hundred miles on it. It's out of the question. Besides, it's too heavy."

"Then we're gonna walk! I'm not risking my snowmobile," he replied.

"Jerry, think about what you're saying. You're willing to risk your life but not your five hundred dollar snowmobile? That doesn't make sense. We have to use your snowmobile because it's light and where I want to go is too far to walk. Anyway, I have a plan. We'll take my new oversized plastic Otter sled. I'm certain we won't get into any trouble, but if we do, my sled is big enough to serve as a boat, so we'll be safe."

Reluctantly, he agreed to take his snowmobile. We drove to the landing, unloaded our gear, and headed out.

On the way out, we checked the ice a couple of times. It was three to four inches thick, which is marginal but generally considered safe. Also, there were other guys fishing so we felt comfortable traveling out at least as far as they were. After we passed the last fisherman, we stopped once again to check the ice. It was still three to four inches thick.

When we got back on the snowmobile, Jerry asked, "How far out are we gonna go?"

"A little farther," I replied.

We moved out cautiously and stopped when we came to a crack that seemed to run across the entire length of the Bay. We decided not to cross the crack.

I set up my portable shelter and started a little propane gas burner to warm it up inside. Pretty soon, I noticed that I was sitting in about an inch and a half of water. I determined it was a result of the combination of my weight plus that of the snowmobile pushing the ice down and allowing it to flood. I moved the snowmobile away from the shelter and although it lowered the amount of water, I still had about an inch in my shelter. It was very slippery and I had to be extremely careful to keep from falling.

The fishing was slow. After an hour, we'd had a couple of bites but hadn't caught any fish.

OUTDOOR FOLLIES

Meanwhile, I wandered over toward the crack. I noticed that it had opened up to about six inches. Must be some sort of pressure crack, I thought. I think I'll put a "tip-up" in the opening.

I started getting bites on the tip-up right away but by the time I ran to it on the slick ice, the fish had already stolen the minnow and was gone.

Because I was getting bites in the crack, I concluded that the fish might be just on the other side of it. Of course, the splake might be up to their old trick of trying to lure me onto thin ice. I leaned across the crack and tested the ice with my ice chisel. It was the same thickness on both sides. "No danger there, the splake must be losing their touch," I thought.

I checked with Jerry and found that he wasn't getting any bites either.

Ideally, we could have set up right on the crack but that was impractical because the crack might open or close slightly causing problems with our shelters. Since it was too cold to fish without a shelter, I suggested that we should cross the crack and set up on the other side. Jerry was a little "iffy" about the idea but agreed to it as long as we left the snowmobile on the safer side. We pulled the sled across and set up our shelters about one hundred yards from the crack.

After setting up my shelter, I found the same problem with water on the ice as I had at the other location. I'd need to be careful to avoid falling. I reached into the minnow pail and plucked out a minnow. As I held it in my hand, preparing to put it on my hook, I thought, "You're the unluckiest minnow in the world." He gave a flip, jumped out of my hand and landed in the hole. "Well," I thought, "I was wrong, you're the luckiest minnow in world." Then I plucked the real unluckiest minnow in the world from the pail, hooked him on my line and dropped him down the hole.

It was only minutes before I had a bite. I set the hook and felt a nice splake. Pulling him carefully to the surface, I managed to reach down and grab him with one hand while removing the hook with the other.

Suddenly, he gave a hard flip, causing me to lose my grip. He flopped on the ice. It's amazing how fast a fish can swim in an inch of water. He zipped to the corner of the shelter and stopped. I jumped off my chair, momentarily forgetting about the water and fell flat on my back in a splat, soaking half my clothing. Regardless, in an adrenaline rush, I sprung to my hands and knees and turned to grab the splake who was now looking at me from the corner of the shelter. He'd look at the hole and then at me and then back at the hole.

"He's going to make a run for it," I thought. Just then, the fish glanced to my left, completely faking me out, and made a run for the hole to my right. In a split second he zipped past me and dove into the hole. I made a grab for him but only succeeded in drenching my arm to the shoulder.

This was war! I knew they were clever but nothing like I had just witnessed. OK, if they wanted to play hardball, that was fine with me.

I got another bite. I let him take it until I was certain he had the bait deep in his mouth and then I set the hook. This one didn't feel as big as the first one. I carefully pulled him to the surface and grabbed him with my left hand. He looked legal but I wasn't certain. He could be one of those fourteen and nine-tenths inchers. I had a board with me that measured exactly fifteen inches. I would use it to measure him.

I tried to hold him still on the board but it was impossible. He was one pound of pure muscle and wasn't going to hold still for anybody. I'd hold his head down on one end of the board with my elbow while trying to get my other hand on his tail and he'd squirm free and flop on the ice. I still had the hook in him so it was only a matter of pulling him back to me for another try. After several tries, all I succeeded in doing was to cover my hands and clothing with slime and fish excrement. A couple of times he held still long enough so I could nearly read the measurement. It appeared that he was a little short, like about one-tenth of an inch short, but I wasn't certain. Perhaps if I pinched his tail he'd make fifteen inches. I'd let go of his head to pinch his tail and just as I was about to get an exact measurement, he'd flop off the board and make a run for the corner of the tent. To heck with it, I decided. I'll give him a little tap on the head to stun him so he'll hold still long enough for me to measure him. Sure enough, nothing like a little rap on the head to slow him down.

I put him on the board and after pinching his tail, I was disappointed to see that he was only fourteen and nine-tenths inches long. Shoot! I had the fish stretcher but I had planned only to use it in case of an emergency, such as hooking a fish deep in the throat that probably would have died anyway. I decided to release him and tossed him into the hole. He just lay there, belly up. I tapped him with my toe but that didn't help. I picked him up and looked at him. He didn't look very healthy, in fact, he looked dead. Perhaps a full swing with an oak club was a little more than I needed to stun him.

I wasn't sure what to do. It would be senseless to stuff a dead fish down the hole. Certainly the warden would understand that this was an accident, wouldn't he? On the other hand, I was concerned; wardens don't have a reputation for being particularly understanding about such matters. I decided to try the fish stretcher.

I secured the splake to the fish stretcher and took a couple of turns on the winch. I stretched the fish until I could hear things breaking, then I measured it again. It was still fourteen and nine-tenths inches. The blasted thing was like a rubber band! I could stretch it out to fifteen inches but when I released the tension he would spring back to his original length. Ridiculous! I decided to gut and gill the fish hoping that might cause it to stretch easier. When I finished, I put it back on the fish stretcher and cranked it as hard as I dared. When I removed it from the fish stretcher, it still returned to its original length. Incredible! I gave it one more try, cranking as hard as I could. POP! To my amazement, I had pulled the head off. Darn! The fish stretcher would have to go back to the drawing board. Regardless, I measured the fish again by placing the severed head next to the body. Now he was over fifteen inches! However, wardens are a notoriously suspicious lot and might wonder about the severed head. I'd better wrap the fish in a plastic bag and hide it in my tackle-box . . . a warden would never think to look in there.

The fishing was pretty good. Jerry and I caught several fish, but they were barely legal. We also caught quite a few that were undersized. I decided not to try my fish stretcher again. I knew there were some nice fish around because I had lost a couple that felt big. I hoped I would catch at least one of those.

    I was fishing two holes in my shelter that were five feet apart. Suddenly, the cork in the right hole went down. I set the hook and felt a nice fish but it got off. I pulled the thirty-foot line to the surface and was about to re-bait when the cork in the other hole went down. I dropped the line I was working on and grabbed the second line. I hooked a dandy! I slowly pulled him to the surface, carefully easing him out of the hole with my free hand. Holding him up with my right hand, I noticed that he was barely hooked. "I was lucky I got him," I thought, "I wonder how long he is?" I grabbed my measuring board and tried to get an idea of his length by observing how much longer he was than the board. It wasn't necessary because he was obviously legal but I couldn't resist. He looked like he would measure a good nineteen inches. While I was looking at the measurement, I lost my concentration and relaxed my grip. Sensing his chance for freedom, he gave a vicious flip and slipped from my hand. He landed on the ice right on top of my two fishing lines, both of which were lying side by side. Spotting the hole, he gave a mighty swirl of his tail, which tangled my lines into an unbelievable mess. He then tore free of the hook, dove in the hole and swam away. It happened so fast I couldn't believe my eyes. I nearly came unglued!

    Jerry was out of bait and wanted to leave but I had two minnows left. "Come on over here for a minute. I think there's another big one down there," I said. "Give me a couple of minutes to see if I can catch him." I dug out a spare fishing pole, baited up and dropped it down. Plunk! The line had barely reached the bottom when a fish grabbed it. I set the hook and felt a monster. Just as I started to pull, he got off. "Blast!" I yelled to Jerry, "that was really a big fish!" I put my hand in the minnow bucket to get the last minnow but he was so frisky I couldn't catch him. I decided to pour some of the water out of the pail so he'd have less room to swim around. I started pouring the water from the pail and the minnow saw his chance for freedom and never looked back. A salmon jumping the Klamath River Falls never looked any more graceful than that minnow when he leaped from the pail to freedom in the hole. "Shoot!" I said, "I know there's a big fish down there and now I don't have any bait!"

"Forget it," Jerry said. "Let's get out of here."

"Wait a second. I can see the minnow under the ice. He's swimming toward the other hole. You tap on the ice behind him and I'll try to catch him with my ice skimmer when he comes through."

It was easy to drive the minnow toward the hole but as soon as I tried to make a grab for him with my ice skimmer, he'd dart away. He was as nervous as a cat. We drove him back to the other hole with the same result. After several tries we gave up. "He's the luckiest minnow in the world!" Jerry said.

"Second luckiest," I replied without elaborating.

We loaded up our gear and walked back toward the crack. When we got to the crack, we were amazed to find that it had opened up to about twelve feet. Apparently the wind had moved the ice on our side of the crack toward open water.

"Holy cow!" Jerry exclaimed. "Look at that! It's a good thing we quit when we did or this crack would be a half mile wide. As it is, I don't know how we're going to get across."

"Not a problem, Jerry," I explained, "that's why I brought this sled. I'll just row myself across and scoot the sled back for you. You gotta get up pretty early in the morning to fool old Pete."

"I don't think so. Why don't I go across and send the sled back for you?"

"Because it's my sled?" I suggested.

"No deal, we'll go across together."

We'd have to float a fair amount of equipment across with us. Perhaps this was going to be a slightly larger problem than I had anticipated.

We loaded the sled with our gear. It floated nicely. Then Jerry got in. It settled about four inches deeper. Since there was now only three inches of freeboard remaining, if I got in, the water would be approximately one inch over the top.

"We got a problem," I said. "If I get in, the sled will sink."

"No, we ain't got a problem. You got a problem," he answered.

"Don't be a wise guy. What do you mean?" I asked.

"I mean, you've stuffed a few too many cookies down your gullet the last fifty years. You weigh a good fifty pounds more than I do. Obviously, we can't cross together. You're so heavy that if you get in this sled with all the equipment, you'll be so low in the water, you'll never make it across. I'll cross first, unload the equipment and send the sled back to you."

"All right. Go ahead, but hurry it up!"

Jerry used my measuring board to paddle. It was slow going and about halfway across the wind picked up.

"Hurry up!" I yelled. "The wind is started to blow harder."

"I'm going as fast as I can. The wind is holding me up."

Just as he reached the other side, the wind picked up to near gale force. The crack was beginning to widen noticeably and I was on the edge of panic.

Jerry removed the gear in what seemed like slow motion while the crack grew wider. When he finished, he shoved the sled back to me. Even with the strong wind, it seemed to take forever to float across to me. By the time I grabbed it and got in, the crack was twenty-five feet across. I looked for the paddle but couldn't find it.

"Jerry!" I yelled. "Where's the @#&%#@ paddle?"

"Oh, sorry, I forgot to put it back in the sled. Here," he said and tossed it toward me. It landed in the water about halfway across and drifted slowly towards me. Finally, I could reach it.

Now I was looking at a sizable amount of open water. I knelt down in the sled and started paddling for all I was worth. The wind was howling and kept turning the sled in circles, making headway difficult. I'll tell you, I had that paddle smoking. It looked like a wheel on a Mississippi River boat. I found that by leaning out the front I could avoid spinning in circles and began to close the gap.

I glanced behind me at the ice on which we had been fishing. It was now picking up steam and heading for parts unknown. "Holy buckets," I thought, "we could have been on that." I also could have sworn I saw splake jumping and splashing with big smiles on their faces. They thought they had me but I fooled them with the sled.

I was now only about fifteen feet from the safe ice but I was having difficulty making headway. For emergencies, I always carry a stick with about thirty feet of rope attached to it. I had previously stuffed it in the storage compartment of Jerry's machine. I yelled to Jerry to get it. He found it, unraveled the rope and tossed the stick to me. I had to stop paddling to grab the stick and immediately started drifting. Jerry held the other end of the rope but when it got tight, it threatened to pull him off his feet because he was standing on glare ice.

"I'm going to have to let go or I'll get pulled in," he yelled.

"If you let go, I'll come back from the grave and strangle you! Now hold on!" I screamed, as I frantically tied the rope to the front of the sled. Jerry pulled and I paddled, and by the skin of our teeth, I made it across.

"Whew! That was close," I said.

"Close? I guess it was close," he answered. "Any closer and I would have had a new sled and shelter. I didn't think you were going to make it. By the way, where do you keep those new golf clubs you bought last summer?"

"Don't worry about those golf clubs. Let's get out of here before another piece breaks off," I answered.

We packed up and made it back to the landing without incident.

Just our luck, when we got to the landing, a warden wandered over to us. "How was the fishing, boys?"

"We got a couple," I answered.

"Mind if I look at them?"

"No, go right ahead," I gulped.

He measured the fish and determined they were all legal. "You know," he went on, "I've been catching a lot of guys with undersized fish. Do you mind if I check your equipment?"

"Um... err... gee, I'm all wet and cold officer, but I suppose it would be alright if you hurry."

He looked through my equipment and then picked up my tackle box. "Wouldn't have a small one in here by any chance, would you?"

"Err. . . ah. . . small one? No, I wouldn't have a small one." He was just about to open the tackle box when he spotted my fish stretcher. Losing interest in the tackle box, he picked up the fish stretcher with a quizzical look on his face. "What the heck is this?"

"That's a . . . a. . . it's a . . . a fish stabilizer," I blurted. "I use it to hold fish still so I can measure them."

"Jeez," he said, shaking his head as he moved away to check the next group of fishermen coming in. "Now I've seen everything."

"Well," I thought. "Perhaps my fish stretcher has a future after all."

THE GREAT BAY
CITY CREEK CANOE RUN

• •

Growing up in the early fifties in the small town of Ashland, Wisconsin, was a dream come true for an adventurous young boy who loved being near water.

Our home was ideally located between Lake Superior, only a few blocks to the north, and Bay City Creek, a few blocks to the south.

The "Crick," as it was known locally, was normally a placid little trickle that you could hop across most of the time. However, like many little creeks, it could become a raging torrent under the right conditions.

Located in the bottom of a large ravine, Bay City Creek was like a magnet to us when we were young. We skied and rode our sleds down the sides of the ravine in the winter and fished and played in the brush around the Creek in the summer.

My mother hated Bay City Creek. She was certain we'd somehow end up getting hurt or drowning in it. We weren't supposed to go near the Crick when the water was high but the allure was too great to resist.

My friend, Billy, lived even closer to the Creek than I did and we often went down there together.

Billy was a member of a family of a dozen children who grew up "wild." He had good parents but they had so many children they were bewildered. Also, what they had in children they lacked in money.

Their house was a shabby affair, more like a cave than a house, with almost no furnishings. In one room there was nothing but a kitchen table and a chair, on which Billy's father was usually seated. I hesitate to call it a kitchen, as there was never any sign of food.

His father was perpetually angry and always had a scowl on his face. He was constantly yelling at one child or another about this thing or that. Another room contained a dirty threadbare couch on which his mother sat watching a black and white television set, which was remarkable because it was probably only one of a dozen television sets in the entire town. It was as though they had pooled all their assets for that single black and white television set.

There were children coming and going constantly, either family members or friends. I was never certain who was who.

Nowadays, we'd probably consider their home environment as abusive, but nobody thought anything of it back then. In fact, their children liked it because they had more freedom than families with only one or two children. I mean, when you have so many children, it's pretty hard to ride herd on any one child for any length of time. Billy's father ruled with an iron fist. He was fair but you really didn't want to get crossways with him. For the most part, none of the children did . . . it was a sort of live and let live. All they had to do was stay out of serious trouble.

Billy was the kind of kid who could do anything. You know the kind: wiry, smart and tough. He also owned things I wasn't allowed to own. Things like a BB gun, bow and arrow and later, a twenty-two rifle. Whenever I'd ask my dad for such stuff, he'd go on a tirade about how I was going to get hurt or put somebody's eye out.

On one beautiful spring day, when the weather had warmed to unseasonable highs and the snow, which only recently had been piled high, had nearly all melted, Billy stopped by my house.

"Hey, Pete," he said, "let's go screw around somewhere."

"Sure," I answered, "I'll tell my folks and be right out."

I told my dad that Billy and I were going outside to play and I'd be back around suppertime. He asked me where I was going and I told him I wasn't certain but we'd probably go over to the ballpark. "Well, all right," he answered, "but stay the hell away from Bay City Creek!"

"Yeah, sure Dad."

Billy and I walked over to the ballpark but the ground was so muddy that nobody else was playing ball.

"What should we do?" he asked.

"Let's go down to the Crick," I replied. "I'll bet it's really roaring."

When we got to the Creek, we found it was even wilder than we had imagined. It looked like the Colorado River at flood stage. Barely within the banks that had been carved out by a previous flood, it was at least eight feet above its normal trickle. It was awesome, frightening to look at as it slammed its way from bend to bend throwing waves up to four feet high in the air. Blood red from the clay that dominates the area, it tumbled downstream in a headlong torrent.

"Wow! Look at that," Billy said. "I've never seen the Crick so high."

"Yeah," I answered, "it's almost all whitewater."

We watched the Creek from a distance but then decided to get closer. Sticking to the high ground, we cautiously worked our way downstream.

Over the years the area through which we walked had served as a convenient place to dump unwanted items. As we were walking along, we stumbled on an old horse trough that somebody had discarded.

"Hey, look at this," Billy said. "It looks like an old boat."

"Naw, it isn't a boat," I replied. "It's an old horse trough."

"That doesn't matter," he said. "It could be a boat, even a canoe. If it was a horse trough, it must have held water. That means it will float like a boat."

"Yeah, I suppose," I agreed. "So what?"

"I'm thinking we could get a hammer and a saw from my dad's garage, put a little deck on this 'boat' and float it over there where the Crick makes that big bend. See? There's a nice quiet eddy. As long we stay away from the main current, we'll be plenty safe," he answered.

"I don't know, Billy. It looks dangerous."

"Aw, you chicken, it isn't dangerous. We'll be careful. Come on, it'll be fun," he said enthusiastically.

"OK," I replied hesitantly.

We hurried back to his father's garage to get a hammer, nails, boards and a saw. While we were looking for the materials, I noticed a kid about three years younger than us, watching from a distance.

"What are you guys doing?" he asked. "Can I help?"

"No!" Billy replied. "Get out of here."

"Who is that kid?" I asked.

"I think he's my brother."

The kid lagged behind a ways but continued to watch as he followed us back to the Creek.

"Go home," Billy said. "It's too dangerous for a little kid where we're going."

"If you can go, I can go. Otherwise, I'm telling Dad you took his tools," he replied.

"You little twerp! If you tell on me, I'll wring your neck. You can come along but stay behind us and out of trouble," Billy answered with a scowl.

We nailed boards across the top for a deck but left a couple of openings so we could sit in the bottom of the boat and paddle. Our paddles were two one-inch pine boards cut to resemble canoe paddles. Finally, we attached a twenty-foot piece of rope to one end of the "canoe," thinking it might be a good idea to tie the canoe off to a tree when we tested it. When we finished, I noticed that our canoe looked an awful lot like a coffin.

We dragged our canoe to the edge of the eddy and were ready to test it but couldn't find a tree to tie it to.

"Hey, Twerp," Billy said. "Com 'ere and hold this rope while we test our canoe."

"I ain't a twerp!" he answered. "My name is Bobby. I'll hold the rope but I don't want you calling me a twerp."

"All right, Twerp," Billy said with an evil grin.

Bobby didn't say anything but I saw a look on his face that told me it wouldn't be wise to push this kid too far.

"Hey, Billy," I whispered. "You better quit needling your brother or he's gonna find a way to get even."

"Hah!" Billy snorted. "I'll take care of him if he gives us

any trouble."

We launched the canoe and got in. We were pleased to find it was surprisingly stable. Bobby held the rope and Billy and I paddled around near the edge of the eddy being careful not to allow the canoe to get caught in the current.

"Hey, this is fun," Billy said. "I told you we could do it," he said as he eased the canoe a little farther into the eddy.

"Be careful, Billy, we're getting pretty close to the main Crick."

"Don't be such a chicken," he said, "come on."

We moved out a little farther into the eddy when suddenly the front of the canoe started to be pulled into the current of the Creek. Frantically, we back-paddled but couldn't get back into the safety of the eddy. It was a good thing Bobby was holding the rope.

"Bobby!" I yelled. "Pull us back."

"Sure," Bobby answered, "as soon as you give me a quarter."

"Give you a quarter?" Billy screeched. "I'll give you a bloody nose you little crook. Now shut up and pull us out of here!"

"Nope, either you give me a quarter or I'll let go of this rope and I'm not going to stand around all day and argue about it."

Bobby wouldn't budge. Regardless of our threats he stuck to his guns. We either had to give him a quarter or he was going to let go of the rope. Fortunately, I had a quarter in my pocket and I tossed it to him. He pocketed the quarter and was about to pull us in when Billy said, "Hurry up about it, you twerp!"

Something dangerous flashed in Bobby's face. He shot his brother a malicious look and said, "Twerp, eh? I warned you not to call me that. Here," he said, throwing the rope to us, "pull yourself in."

"Holy SH............!" I screamed. "Paddle for your life Billy."

Our paddles were churning the water into a froth but to no avail. Slowly, inexplicably, we were pulled into the churning whitewater of Bay City Creek.

Once we started down the Creek, we could do little to control the canoe except to keep the front pointing downstream. Frantically, paddling for all we were worth, we were able to keep the canoe from turning sideways. It was unbelievable. There was whitewater everywhere. One minute we were on top of a rushing wave and the next we were practically underwater. The Creek slammed us from bank to bank drenching us with gallons of water, but somehow, someway, our little craft managed to stay upright and headed, bow first, down the Creek.

"Paddle for shore! Paddle for shore!" Billy yelled, as we barreled down the Creek at breakneck speed, but it was hopeless. We would come tantalizingly close to one bank only to be swept back into the channel headed for the other bank. All of a sudden Billy let out a terrified scream, "Pete! Oh no! We're going to be sucked into the Tunnel!"

The "Tunnel," as it was known locally, was a sandstone block tunnel constructed many years ago over the creek. Its purpose was to protect the footings of a railroad bridge that also spanned the Creek. Normally, the Creek would flow gently through the Tunnel with ten to fifteen feet of clearance to the ceiling, but today would be different. Today there would be a raging torrent of water cascading down a long straightaway into the Tunnel, with barely enough clearance for our boat and us. The Tunnel was long, at least one hundred feet, and to make matters worse, we wouldn't be able to see. It would be pitch black and we would be completely at the mercy of the Creek. Terrified, we realized there was nothing we could do; we would have to run the Tunnel.

As we were hurtled down the straight stretch before the Tunnel, it was like looking death straight in the eye. The angry maw that was the Tunnel entrance looked like the mouth of a vicious animal, swallowing anything that came its way.

Billy and I both attended St. Agnes Catholic School. We might not have been model religion students, but I assure you that, as we were staring at the mouth of the Tunnel, the Hail Marys and Act of Contritions were "flying." With eyes as wide as saucers, both of us screaming for help that wasn't going to come, we were swallowed by the Tunnel.

I decided I would take it like a man . . . screaming, with my eyes clenched tightly shut. Then, when we didn't immediately capsize and drown, I tentatively opened them. It was unbelievable! Completely and totally black! The sound of cascading water, which was magnified by the echo effect of the Tunnel, was like a thousand screaming demons from hell. At that moment I was certain I was going to die, either from drowning or fright.

Then I saw it! A thin sliver of light at the other end of the Tunnel.

"Keep it in the center of the Creek!" I screamed. "I can see light at the other end!" Incredibly, lovingly, we were spit out of the Tunnel like a shot from a cannon.

After the Tunnel, everything was anticlimactic. The Creek continued its headlong rush for another couple of hundred yards but then went over its banks and flooded the entire area. We were able to paddle out of the main channel to dry land. The great Bay City Canoe Run was over.

"Wow!" Billy said. "That was quite a ride. I'd like to try it again but I got a little brother that needs tending to."

"If I were you, I'd leave him alone. He's not the type of kid to mess with," I answered. "Anyway, if you wanna run it again, run it with somebody else. I gotta go home and change pants, and it ain't just because they're wet."

THE EDUCATION
OF A TURKEY HUNTER

••••••••••••••••••••••••••

Last Tuesday while playing cards at our local Elks Lodge, I remarked to the other players that I had just returned from an exhausting turkey hunt in southern Wisconsin.

"Did you get a turkey?" Bill asked.

"Yeah," I answered, "but it was a tough hunt!"

"Tough?" Doc said. "I can't understand why. What's so difficult in bringing about the demise of a bird that has a brain so small it's almost in the class of the Dodo bird? After all, when you compare the size of their brain to the rest of their body, they're among the least mentally endowed of all bird species. Their cranium is just too small to contain enough brain matter for performing basic functions such as seeing, hearing, walking, flying and finding food, to allow enough remaining brain matter to be dedicated to developing a sophisticated means of avoiding hunters. It's amazing they're not extinct. I mean, if they had the same amount of brains relative to size as a mouse, their heads would be the size of a basketball. As you know, I don't hunt but I believe that even the dumbest hunter would have an easy time outsmarting a turkey."

"What the heck did Doc just say?" Bill asked.

"He said turkeys were stupid," Jerry answered.

Doc, a local physician, wasn't a hunter but tended to think he was an expert on every subject.

Bill, was a very shrewd businessperson. When he spoke, you'd wonder how he made it through second-grade English; but those of us who knew him well understood that he was a very smart guy. You seldom got the better of Bill.

"Tell you what, Doc," Bill said. "I'll bet you a case of Scotch that you can't kill a turkey."

"I'm sorry, Bill, I'd like to take you up on that bet but as you know, I don't hunt."

"That don't matter none, Doc. You must have a video camera. You jus' take that camera and get me a good picture of a tom turkey up close, let's say forty yards, and you win. They ain't as dumb as you think. I hunted 'em once and I only seen one bird."

"Well, that is a tempting offer. I don't have a camera but I could use my wife's. Ordinarily, I wouldn't even ask her as she spent months looking at cameras, checking features and prices before finally buying one. It's an extremely expensive professional model, you know. She'd never let me touch it but she's out of town right now and when the cat's away, the mice will play. Heh heh heh," he chuckled. "Fair enough, if Pete will guide me, I'll take your bet."

" Pete's gonna guide you? Let's make it two cases," Bill said.

"Wise guy," I answered. "I'll guide Doc and it's going to cost you two cases of good Scotch!"

I arranged to meet Doc the following Friday afternoon. He owned a Lincoln Navigator but when I suggested we use it for the trip, he got nervous. "I don't mind driving but I never take my vehicles off the blacktop. Are the roads all blacktopped down there?"

"Vehicle? It might be fancy but it's just a truck to me. Yeah, we can stay on blacktop as long as we're willing to walk a short distance to the hunting area."

"Well . . . OK, but we're going to have to be careful. That vehicle is very expensive and I take very good care of it."

When Doc picked me up, I had my shotgun with me.

"Why are you bringing a gun?" he asked.

"There are still a few turkey tags left over from the draw and I thought you might get so excited about turkey hunting you'll want to buy a license."

He frowned at me. "Really, Pete, I thought you knew me better than that. I am morally opposed to hunting. Go ahead and throw the gun in the vehicle. It'll save us the time of hauling it back to your house but I'll guarantee you, I'm never going to use it."

Things started going bad right away. As soon as we left town, we drove into one of those freaky little late-season snowstorms that often visit northern Wisconsin in April. The county snowplow solved the slippery road conditions by dumping tons of salt. "Good grief!" Doc complained. "Haven't these people ever heard of a snowplow? My vehicle is getting covered with salt . . . I never drive it when there's salt on the road. We'll have to have it washed as soon as possible."

"Whatever. Wake me up when we get there. It's slippery out there so be careful," I warned him.

I fell asleep, but was suddenly jolted awake. Looking out the windshield, I was amazed. "Wow!" I exclaimed, "It's really nasty out there. I think I'll stay awake for a while. I can't sleep anyway. I keep having a nightmare about sliding over an embankment."

"It wasn't a nightmare," Doc said through clenched teeth. "We've nearly slid over an embankment at least a half dozen times. This is insane. We should pull over."

Doc looked a little ragged all right. His white-knuckled fists were clamped to the wheel in a death grip, looking for all the world as though he'd have to have them pried off with a crowbar. It was a sure bet that he'd need to sand his fingerprints off the wheel. His eyes were as big as silver dollars. Even in the dark I could see he was terrified. I thought it was because he's afraid to drive in a snowstorm. I, on the other hand, not encumbered by such phobias, thought nothing of driving the legal speed limit during a howling blizzard. True, on a few occasions, circumstances had resulted in a total loss of my vehicle, not to mention nearly my life. Regardless, I thought I'd relieve his anxiety by offering to drive.

"This is nothing, Doc. I've driven through a dozen storms worse than this. Why don't you pull over and let me drive."

"Let you drive? Let you drive?" Doc screamed. "I wouldn't let you touch this wheel if it meant we had to spend the rest of our lives waiting for a snowplow. Your driving ability, rather I should say, lack of driving ability, is legendary. How many trucks have you totaled so far? How many trips to the emergency room have you made? You're crazy if you think I'd let you touch this wheel."

"OK Doc, it's your call but we're not going to get there until late."

"I'd just as soon get there late as not at all."

After another fifty miles, the snow turned to rain and eventually quit. We arrived at our motel around ten p.m. It was midnight before we got organized and ready for bed. I told Doc I'd wake him up in the morning.

At 2:45 a.m. I was pounding on Doc's door. "Come on Doc, get up! It's time to go."

I pounded and pounded. Finally I could hear him stumbling around in the dark banging into things and muttering about finding a light switch. Fighting his way to the door, he opened it and said, "My God! What's wrong? Is there a fire?"

"Fire? Huh? No, there's nothing wrong. It's time to go hunting."

"Are you insane? It's three in the morning."

"Doc, our best chance is first thing in the morning. It gets daylight at quarter to five and if we don't get moving right now we're going to be late."

Doc was extremely ill-tempered during the drive to the hunting location. He spent the entire time complaining that he had no idea he'd have to freeze his butt off stumbling through the brush in the dead of night just to videotape a stupid turkey.

"Doc," I said, "I'm getting tired of your whining. You wanted me to guide you and that's what I'm doing, so dry up."

"Well, yes, I suppose you are but I wish you would have been a little more explicit about what would be involved," he said.

"I believe in self-discovery," I said as I prodded him out the truck door into the cold, still morning.

"Boy, it's dark out here, Pete. I can't see my hand in front of my face."

"Yeah, it's dark all right. That's OK though, I know exactly where we're going. We'll walk up this little valley for a quarter mile or so and then climb the ridge to our left. I know a shortcut, I remember it from the last time I was here."

Doc had never been with me on one of my shortcuts. If he had, he would have known that I've taken shortcuts that have resulted in my getting out of the woods several hours after dark. I felt no need to trouble him with any details of those prior shortcuts.

We started up the valley and hadn't made much headway before Doc was puffing pretty hard.

"Hey, Doc, you ought to start taking some of that advice you've been dishing out to your patients the last twenty years and lose a little weight."

"Yeah . . . how did I know we'd be climbing a mountain?"

"Mountain? Heck, this is the flat part. Wait till we start climbing the ridge."

Once we were a quarter mile up the valley we turned left and started to ascend the ridge. Daylight was just starting to break and we could make out the dark shapes of trees.

Doc was facing the ridge we were about to climb and said, "What is this? It isn't a ridge, it's a cliff! I can reach out in front of me and touch the ground with my hand."

"Yeah, it's steep here," I agreed. "But as soon as we climb a little higher, it'll get easier. We'll take our time and work our way up on an angle. Once we get to the top, there's a good chance we'll find some turkeys."

"Ridge! It's a cliff! We can't climb it, we'll die!" Doc gasped, nearly out of breath.

"We have to climb it, Doc." I said in an exasperated voice, "It's where the turkeys are. If we don't climb it, Bill is going to win that bet and I don't want him to win! I'm still mad about a Packer bet he beat me on ten years ago. We'll take our time and before you know it we'll be on the top."

We started up. It was a tough climb but we worked our way up slowly. I had to stop several times for Doc, who was constantly slipping and sliding, virtually pulling himself up from tree to tree. I thought I knew where we were going, but nothing looked the same as I remembered it. As we worked our way along, it seemed as though the terrain was getting steeper. I had visions of Doc tumbling down the hillside, or even worse, me tumbling down the hillside.

"Oh my God!" Doc moaned. "I can't go much farther. I must

have been out of my mind to come up here with you."

I had to agree, it was tough going but I kept moving, thinking it would level off.

"Pete!" Doc whispered. "I'm getting frightened. If we fall, we're not going to stop until we hit the bottom. What the heck have you gotten me into?"

The slope had slowly become a limestone cliff and we were walking on a narrow little trail that angled slightly toward the top. Even I was getting scared . . . which meant we were in deep trouble.

"I must have missed the spot I was looking for, but we don't have any choice now. It would be more dangerous to go back than to continue forward. Let's keep edging our way along, I think we'll find a spot where we can climb to the top. Don't look down," I advised.

"Don't worry! I'm scared to death of heights. If we ever get out of this, I'm never, I repeat NEVER, going to get involved in anything with you again."

I glanced over at Doc. He was a sight. His face was as white as a ghost and dripping with sweat.

We continued to inch our way along when, miraculously, the cliff gave way to a gentler ascent to the top. Suddenly, about three hundred yards from the top, we heard our first gobble.

"What was that?" Doc whispered.

"A turkey," I answered.

"Good! Where is he? Let's go videotape him and get out of this nightmare."

"It's not that easy. He's all the way up on the top of the ridge. He won't come down to our call. We'll have to climb to the same level he's on before I try to call him," I explained.

"Good grief, whatever! I made it this far; I suppose I can make it the rest of the way," Doc huffed.

We climbed to the top and as I was looking for a good location to call from, Doc suggested we move closer.

"No," I said. "We might scare him."

"That's nonsense. The closer we get, the better chance we have of calling him," Doc answered. "I heard him gobble just a minute ago and he was at least two hundred yards away. He could never see us from that far away. Let's just go over this knoll . . ."

As he popped his head over the knoll I heard the distinctive "putt, putt, putt" of an alarmed turkey and the next thing we knew, the bird was flying off his roost down into the valley on the opposite side of the ridge.

"Blast!" Doc said. "We were two hundred yards from him; it isn't even full daylight. How the heck did he see us?"

"They got good eyes, Doc."

We walked along the ridge and tried calling from various locations. After several tries we heard a very distant gobble.

"There!" Doc said, "another one."

"Yeah," I answered, "let's go after him." Then I started down the ridge.

"Where are you going?" Doc asked.

"That turkey answered from the opposite ridge. We'll have to cross the valley to the ridge on the other side."

"What? Are you crazy? We just got up here!" He exclaimed.

"We frightened the turkey that was up here. The only bird we have a chance at is on the other ridge. We have to cross."

"My God . . . this is worse than a nightmare. I don't know if I can make another climb like this," he said.

"You can do it, Doc. It's daylight now and we'll be able to pick a better spot to climb down. We'll just take it a little at a time."

We descended to the valley floor and started climbing the other ridge. Doc was getting a little ragged around the edges but a couple of cases of Scotch were a strong motivating factor and he started the climb.

We were able to find a more gentle slope and slowly made our ascent. Even though this was an easier climb, Doc was continually winded, constantly gasped for breath and stopped frequently. All this resulted in a slower ascent than I would have liked. As we climbed, we could hear a turkey gobbling several hundred yards away.

Just before we reached the top, the bird stopped gobbling. That meant he was on the move.

"I think he's moving. We'd better set up right now," I said quickly. "Get your camera ready and put your face-mask on."

"Oh blast! I forgot my facemask in my vehicle. To heck with it! I don't need it. This timber is wide open. If you can get that bird within a hundred yards, I'll use my telephoto lens. He'll be so far away, he'll never see us."

"I don't know, Doc. These birds are very wary."

"He can't possibly see me if I don't move. I'll have the camera all set and as soon as I see the bird, I'll start taping."

Doc got his camera ready and sat by a large tree. I gave a few soft yelps and almost instantly the turkey gobbled. Suddenly, like a ghost, there he was! I glanced at Doc, who saw the bird at the same time as I did, and could see that he had come down with an instant case of turkey fever. His mouth dropped open and his eyes bugged out at the sight of the turkey. Just as he was about to start filming, the turkey suddenly let out an alarm putt and ran off.

"What happened? I never moved a muscle," Doc screeched.

"Your mouth fell open." I answered.

"My mouth fell open? My mouth fell open? Are you telling me that bird saw me open my mouth from one hundred and fifty yards?"

"They got good eyes, Doc."

It had been cloudy all morning and now it started to rain. One of those slow, misty, cold spring rains. I reached into my fanny pack and pulled out my rain gear.

"Where's your rain gear, Doc?" I inquired.

"In the vehicle."

"Is there anything you didn't leave in the vehicle?" I asked sarcastically.

We had no choice; we had to go back to the vehicle for his rain gear. It was just as well, because any turkeys on the ridge were already alerted and those that weren't would certainly be working their way toward their strutting area, which was at the head end of the valley.

OUTDOOR FOLLIES

The descent was tricky, as the slope had become very slick in the rain. Doc's boots were designed for a flat surface and he struggled to keep his footing as we slipped and stumbled our way to the bottom. The temperature was barely above freezing and he was wet and getting very cold.

"How much farther is it, Pete? I'm freezing."

"Not too far, about a mile."

"A mile? I'll never make it!"

"You're gonna have to make it, cause I ain't carrying you," I answered.

Doc started shivering so hard he could barely talk.

"I'm c c c old! I'm s s s uffering f f f rom h h h hypothermia," Doc stammered.

"Aw, it's all in your head. Just pretend you're warm and you'll be fine," I answered.

Thinking I could help him by getting his mind off his dilemma, I added, "By the way, you might want to invest in one of these newly developed rain jackets like the one I'm wearing. I do believe it's one of the best rain jackets I've ever had. Why, I'm not only dry, I'm also comfortable . . . not too warm, not too cold."

My strategy worked better than I thought. Almost too well as Doc flew into what only could be described as a hypothermic rage.

His face got red and I actually thought I saw steam spurting from his ears. Glaring at me with a maniacal look he said, "You jerk! You incredible uncaring jerk! I'm nearly freezing and you're telling me how warm you are in your new raingear. We ought to have the United Nations send you as a goodwill ambassador to some starving third-world nation. I'd love to hear the motivational speech you'd make while stuffing yourself with a seven-course meal. You are a world-class jerk!"

"Jeez, Doc, you don't have to get all huffy. I was just trying to help. Anyway, here we are, I can see your truck just ahead."

Doc got his truck started. After he warmed up, had some coffee and a candy bar, his mood improved to the point where he could at least speak civilly.

"I've had it with this turkey hunting! I don't care if I lose to Bill.

This vehicle is a total mess. It's full of salt and now we're getting mud all over the seats and floor mats. I'm not sure I'll ever get it clean. I've got aches, cuts and bruises on muscles I didn't know existed and I nearly died from hypothermia. This is the trip from hell . . . there isn't anything else that could happen that hasn't. I've had it! I'm out of here!"

Well, I did have to agree that the trip wasn't everything it could have been; but, hey, was that my fault?

After he warmed up a little more, his disposition improved slightly and I dared to venture a question. "Wanna give it one more try?" I asked.

"What? Climb another cliff, risk my life again? No thanks!" he answered.

"No," I replied. "This will be a gentleman's hunt. Of course, you'll have to be willing to drive your truck a mile or so up a sand road. But I think we'll have a good chance for a turkey. You remember that road we walked on this morning on the way up the valley? It goes all the way to the top of the ridge. Just before the top of the ridge there's an open area where the turkeys like to display. We'll drive up to within a quarter mile and sneak up to that area."

"What do you mean a road to the top of the ridge?" he snorted. "What ridge?"

"The same ridge we climbed, only farther down the ridge."

"What? You mean there's a road up to that ridge and you had me risk my life by climbing it?" he asked incredulously.

"You didn't wanna get your truck dirty," I answered.

"You idiot! My vehicle was already full of salt; what difference would it make? Do you really think that I would risk my life climbing a cliff rather than getting my vehicle dirty?" he screamed.

"There you go, Doc, getting ugly again. You're the one who didn't want mud on your vehicle."

He steamed for a while, then, after some thought said, "Well, if it's that easy, I suppose we could give it one last try."

The rain that had been falling steadily turned the road, which at first appeared to be mostly sand but now was looking more like mud, into a quagmire. Doc put the truck into four-wheel drive and slowly clawed his way up the valley. Suddenly we came to a large, water-filled, muddy spot in the road.

"This spot looks pretty bad, Pete. I wonder if we can make it through?"

"Yeah . . . I've gone through a million worse spots. Just give it a little gas and ease it in."

"All right, I'll try it," Doc answered.

Doc's idea of "easing it in" apparently meant to plunge the accelerator to the floor causing the truck to leap forward into the center of the mud hole. In a heartbeat, he had the truck buried. He tried backing up, but without a push it was hopeless.

"Oh great! Now we are screwed. I must have been insane to come down here with you. What are we going to do now?" he moaned.

"Not to worry. I think we can back out of here because it's slightly downhill but we'll need a little push," I replied.

"Good. Get out and give me a push," he said.

"No can do, Doc. My back is shot. If I try pushing this truck, I'll spend a week in the hospital. You know that. Remember the 'hippopotamus' oath . . . first do no wrong. You'll have to do the pushing."

Doc didn't like the idea of pushing but I had him on a technicality. He knew my back was bad and as I was his patient, he really couldn't recommend that I do anything that might further injure it. It was either let me drive while he pushed, or we weren't going anywhere.

Grudgingly, he got out and waded into the knee-high mud and water. I rolled the window down and on a count of three, he pushed and I floored the accelerator.

The results were nothing short of spectacular. I wouldn't have believed how much mud and water those spinning tires could throw into the air. It was like dropping a dump truck of chocolate pudding into a huge fan. Incredible! One minute we were stuck and the next there was an explosion of mud and water and I was able to slowly inch the vehicle back to solid ground.

I'd lost sight of Doc during the festivities but I thought I could hear him screaming. No doubt screams of joy about our success in freeing his truck. When I did see him, however, he didn't look joyful. I didn't recognize him at first . . . I thought it was some sort of monster we'd just liberated from the swamp hole. He had no recognizable sign of clothing; just a mud-dripping creature with two eyes and a mouth from which emanated language I hadn't heard since I was in the Navy. Creature or no creature, I knew a murderous look when I saw one and for a minute I feared for my life. Fortunately, the creature, which I now recognized as Doc, was so muddy he was reluctant to reach into his precious truck to grab me.

"YOU NITWIT! LOOK WHAT YOU'VE DONE TO ME!" he screamed.

"Gee, Doc, I'm sorry. But you should have known enough not to stand directly in front of a spinning tire. Don't worry, we'll get you cleaned up in no time."

What a grouch. It's a good thing I'd never taken him along on some of the bad trips I've made. Getting him cleaned up meant yet another entire change of clothing; lucky he brought plenty of extra clothing with him.

He managed to get changed and back into the warm truck. He was still in a murderous rage but kept it under control. "Let me tell you something, Crowley. You WILL pay for this. I don't know how; I don't know where, but you will pay. Now let's get the hell out of here!"

"Don't you want to walk up and take a look to see if there are any turkeys in the strutting zone?"

He didn't answer. He just jumped in the truck and started driving like a maniac for town.

"What are you doing?" I asked.

"I'm driving to town. I want to see if I can get a deal on a couple cases of Scotch."

He didn't even slow down when he hit the blacktop, just skidded onto the surface and headed for town.

As we were barreling down the road heading to town, incredibly, I noticed a tom turkey standing a short distance away. He was standing between the road and a set of railroad tracks that parallel the road.

"Look at that!" I said. "There's a turkey right there! We could probably get him if we drive a couple of hundred yards past him and sneak back through the woods."

"Forget it!" Doc shouted. "Turkeys are diabolical birds, I give up."

"Jeez, Doc, this is a great opportunity. Tell you what, let's make a try for him and if we don't get him, I'll go fifty/fifty on the Scotch."

It didn't take Doc long to recognize a win-win situation. He slammed on the brakes and turned onto a little side road about two hundred yards from the bird.

"OK," he agreed, "let's try for him."

We got out of the vehicle and began getting our gear together. Doc took his video camera out of the bag and placed it on top of the vehicle while he dug out his facemask and jacket. While he was putting his jacket on, I pushed the door closed rather than slamming it and when doing so, moved the vehicle ever so slightly. That's all it took. The slight curvature of the roof, combined with a plastic case lubricated with rainwater, caused the camera to slip over the edge of the roof. I didn't like the sound it made when it hit the ground.

"My wife's camera!" Doc hissed.

He snatched it up and we saw the lens was cracked. "Oh my God! The lens is broken. I'm a dead man. She will kill me!"

"Calm down, calm down, I'm sure you can replace that lens. If you have it over-nighted you'll have it before she returns from her trip. She'll never know. Trust me, I'm an expert in these matters," I said.

"You? An expert in marital matters? I thought you were just recently divorced?" he snorted.

"I was. And for about sixty percent of everything I owned, I learned about all my marital deficiencies. Now I know better," I answered.

"You don't understand. She spent months researching this camera. It's her pride and joy. When she finds out I took this camera and broke the lens, she'll kill me. And, as far as trusting you . . . after this trip, I'd sooner trust a maniac than you. I'll never trust you again!" he replied.

Just then the turkey started gobbling. He gobbled over and over.

"Listen to that diabolical swine! He probably has some obscure sense in that piss ant brain of his that tells him I just broke my camera! That does it! To hell with it! Give me that shotgun. I'm going to blast that turkey," Doc hissed.

"You can't shoot that turkey, Doc," I said, "you don't have a license."

"Screw the license!" he whispered angrily, "I'll buy one when we get to town." Now give me that gun!"

I didn't like the look in his eye but I gave him the gun anyway. He's a big boy, he knew what he was doing.

We slowly crept down the logging road watching very carefully for the turkey that continued to sound off every few minutes. Sure enough, there he was, in full strut about a hundred yards ahead and just fifty feet or so from the road on the other side of the railroad tracks.

"There he is," I said. "There's a perfect way to sneak up on him. I'll stay here and you follow the railroad tracks, staying out of sight. See that little white pine right by him? When you see the top of that tree, you'll know you're directly abreast of the turkey. I'll stay here where I can watch both you and the turkey, and as soon as you're ready to shoot, but before you show yourself over the railroad bed, I'll yelp. That will distract the turkey and will give you your chance. Shoot fast because you won't have much time. Be careful that there isn't a car on the road."

I was proud of Doc . . . the way he sneaked along that railroad bed like an old pro, never once showing himself. As he reached the white pine, he slowly worked his way out of the ditch to the top of the railroad bed, apparently without making a sound, as the turkey kept turning and displaying. I yelped, Doc shot and a conservation warden tapped me on the shoulder.

"The mechanical decoy your buddy just shot at belongs to the Department of Natural Resources. Is he aware he's not supposed to shoot within fifty yards of the centerline? Have you got anything to say?"

"Yeah. I just lost a case of Scotch. Do you know anybody who can give me a ride to Ashland?"

A MEMORABLE DUCK HUNT

••••••••••••••••••••••••••••••

Most of the stories in this book are humor based on fact. This story is not humorous; it is entirely factual. I included it in this collection because of the historical significance of the storm during which this hunt occurred.

Pete Crowley

I loved duck hunting. I lived for it. I was either hunting ducks, preparing to hunt ducks or thinking about hunting ducks almost every month of the year. During the winter I would repair and repaint my decoys. During the summer I worked on my boat and my blind, and during the fall I hunted . . . almost every day. In between I read about ducks, decoys, decoy spreads and duck hunting. I could identify every species in hand and most in flight. Overall, I was about as crazy about duck hunting as it's possible to be. I hunted ducks almost every day of the season for twenty-five years before slowly drifting away from the sport. I don't do much duck hunting anymore but I still buy a license and duck stamp every year. Regardless, I'll never forget what it was like. The early mornings, snow and freezing temperatures, fall storms, flocks of teal dancing over the bog and the sight and sound of late-season bluebills with their wings cupped coming into the decoys. Over the years I had some great hunts but one late-fall hunt stands out far above the others. This story is about that hunt.

Up here, in northern Wisconsin, the local ducks migrate shortly after the season opens and the majority of the northern ducks have passed through on their way south by November 1st. Regardless, I would never quit hunting until the season ended in late November because there was always a chance for a few golden eyes, buffle heads or late-season mallards.

Peter F. Crowley

The year, 1975 was an unusual year. Although the duck population nationwide was high, the weather was mild and the numbers of migrating ducks passing through northern Wisconsin were low. The hunting was pretty slow in October and after November 1st most of the local hunters had assumed the duck migration was over and gave up. I didn't. I continued to hunt because I thought the majority of the ducks were still in Canada. I was certain that a late-season storm would cause millions of ducks to migrate.

I did most of my duck hunting in the Kakagon Sloughs area, located at the east end of Lake Superior's Chequamegon Bay. Locally, everybody refers to the Kakagon Sloughs, as the "Sloughs." The Sloughs, fed by Wood and Bear Trap creeks, is a huge area of many square miles that can be accessed from the Bay when the weather is decent or from a landing upstream on Bear Trap Creek if the weather is bad.

On November 8th a strong storm system began developing in the western United States. As it moved into the Plains toward the upper Great Lakes, it gained strength and developed into one of the strongest storms on record. This was a killer storm, the same kind of storm that took the lives of nine duck hunters in the upper Mississippi River valley during the great Armistice Day storm of 1940. I lived to hunt ducks in such a storm. I thought I was prepared for it and had every intention of hunting during this one.

The storm moved through our area on November 9th, 10th, and 11th. The first day, November 9th, we had torrential rain, temperatures in the forties and an ENE wind of twenty-five to thirty-five MPH. Such a wind is offshore at Brush Point, the northwesternmost point of land at the mouth of the Sloughs, where I intended to hunt.

I would have preferred to launch my boat in the Bay and follow the shoreline to the mouth of the Sloughs because it's easier than running the Sloughs in the dark, but the wind was so strong and the water so rough it would have been too risky. Instead, I decided to launch upstream on Bear Trap Creek and navigate my way through the Sloughs to Brush Point. This can be tricky; in fact, if you don't know your way around, it's possible to get lost in the Sloughs in full

OUTDOOR FOLLIES

daylight. When it's dark, they're a nightmare! Everything looks the same. It's easy to run into the bog or get confused and make a wrong turn. If that happens and you lose your point of reference, you can run up a dead end or halfway back to the landing before you realize your mistake. Also, because running lights tend to impair vision, some guys didn't use them if there was any moon or starlight to navigate by so there was always the danger of a collision.

My fourteen-foot aluminum boat equipped with an eighteen horsepower motor was a good boat. I had been through a lot of rough water with it and I was confident it could handle the storm. I'd loaded it carefully, making certain I wasn't overweight but still had enough weight to be properly balanced. To find my way in the dark, I had a 500,000 candlepower spot/floodlight powered by a twelve-volt car battery.

I put in at 3:30 a.m. It was pitch black, raining so hard I couldn't see fifty yards; and even in the narrow slough, the wind and rain were whipping the water into a froth. I wondered if I should wait for daylight but then decided to leave right away. Just as I started, a large tree cracked and fell somewhere nearby, but in the dark and with the rain I couldn't tell where, except that it was close. It made me nervous but fortunately there were only trees for the first half mile or so. After that, I would be running entirely through sloughs which flowed through several thousand acres of wild rice beds, bog marshes and low cranberry brush.

This was not a day for mistakes. If I missed the slough channel and ran into the bog on the windward side, I would be stranded because no matter how hard I rowed or poled, I would not be able to gain any headway against such a strong wind. Therefore, I was extremely careful. Regardless, I still had constant trouble. I had trouble staying in the channel, got lost once and was lucky I didn't get stranded in the bog. It was a real nail-biter. Finally, with the help of my light, I battled my way slowly and carefully all the way to Brush Point.

By the time I got there, even though I was wearing rain gear, I was soaked and getting cold. It was still an hour before legal shooting hours so all I could do was set the decoys and huddle in the corner of my gunnysack blind to wait for daylight. Finally, darkness gave way to gray and then to full daylight. I expected to see hundreds of ducks but there was nothing flying, well, almost nothing. I did see a single bluebill cross my decoys but I couldn't get a shot. Soaked and half frozen, I picked up my decoys and headed home. What a disappointment!

It continued to rain and blow all that day and into the night. I called a couple of friends to see if they would be interested in hunting with me the next morning but there were no takers. I was certain this storm would drive some ducks south so I decided to go alone. The wind increased to thirty to forty MPH during the evening and shifted slightly to the ENE, which meant it was blowing parallel to the shoreline from Brush Point to the boat landing in the Bay. Because I had so much trouble running the Sloughs the first day, I decided to take a look at the Bay landing in the morning and then decide whether or not to run the Lake. I also planned to dress warmer and pack a second set of clothing.

Again, I was at the landing at 3:30 a.m. The wind was screaming along the shoreline so strong it was actually raining horizontally. It was impossible to see very far, even with my powerful light. The landing was protected by a breakwall so it was difficult to see how rough the Lake was, but it appeared as though the wind was parallel to the shore. I decided to take a chance and run the Lake. Bad decision!

I launched the boat, got the motor started and turned on my light to take a look. Because of the wind and rain I couldn't see very far. I also found that the light robbed me of my night vision so I decided to turn it off, reasoning that I could initially guide myself by the parking lot light at the landing and then follow the tree line along shore to work my way east toward Brush Point. I still hadn't been able to get a clear look at the water outside the breakwall but from what I could see, it looked rough but navigable.

When I cleared the breakwater, I was shocked at the size of the seas. Even though the wind was blowing along the shoreline, because of the several mile reach to Brush Point it had whipped the Lake into a frenzy. I should have turned around right then but I wasn't certain I could without taking a wave over the transom and swamping the boat. All I could do was keep the bow into the waves and move slowly along the shoreline. It was a wild ride. Once, I turned on the light but the waves were so frightening that I quickly turned it off. The waves and rain were lashing my face and it was almost impossible to keep the tree line in sight. I had to constantly adjust toward shore and occasionally got so close that I got into breakers; in fact, once I got in so close that I felt the skeg hit the bottom in the trough of a wave. Thank God for that seaworthy little boat and a bailing can. I took my time, avoided panic and slowly worked my way east. The closer I got to Brush Point, the smaller the waves were. Eventually I made it. It was the most frightening ride I've ever had in a boat. One thing was certain, I wasn't going home the same way.

Thanks to the second set of dry clothing, I was better off than the day before. Regardless, it didn't take long before I started getting wet and cold. Just before daylight, I set my decoys and waited. Because of the severe storm, I was certain the ducks would be flying. To my amazement, once again, there were no ducks! Could it be that the ducks had migrated earlier in the season? I didn't think so, but where were they? I couldn't believe it. I stayed for a couple of hours until I was thoroughly soaked and then picked up my decoys. I was afraid to venture back on the Lake, so I motored up the Sloughs to the Bear Trap Creek landing and bummed a ride to my truck and trailer from a friend.

Later that day, the temperature dropped to the mid-thirties and it began to snow and sleet. The wind shifted to the WNW and increased to forty to fifty MPH with higher gusts. It was the wildest storm I'd ever seen. In fact, at 7:30 p.m. that evening, still unknown to the outside world, the oar carrier Edmund Fitzgerald sank.

I set the alarm for 2:30 a.m. and went outside. It was wild. The wind was screaming from the WNW and the temperature had dropped to thirty-three degrees Fahrenheit but the snow had nearly stopped. I had the feeling that the storm was passing and today would be the day the ducks would fly. I decided to go.

I launched my boat in Bear Trap Creek. Before I got into the boat, I took a look around. Although it had quit snowing, conditions were extreme. The wind was screaming and had whipped the water into a froth. The trees were snapping back and forth and every so often I could hear one break off and crash to earth. Even in the protected area of the launch site the water looked frightening. I knew these were extremely dangerous conditions and I wondered if I should reconsider hunting that day. In the end, it was no contest, my drive to hunt ducks under stormy conditions easily overcame my fear and I decided to go.

At least there was no rain to contend with and I was able to wear my snowmobile suit so I was dressed as warmly as I could be. My plan was to take it slow and easy, hugging the windward side of the Sloughs and work my way toward Brush Point.

As I started off, I noticed that the storm had caused an unusual current in the Creek and that the water was much higher than usual. I was OK in the wooded area but what would the Sloughs be like farther down where there were no trees and no banks to contain the high water? I soon found out; they were flooded. It was like the entire area was one large lake. In fact, there was so much open water in the Sloughs that the waves were sizable. Fortunately, I could still see enough weeds and brush to follow the channel.

I navigated carefully and slowly, knowing that if I were blown out of the channel and into the bog, I wouldn't be able to get out by myself. I'd run these Sloughs hundreds of times in the dark so I was able to stay oriented and work my way toward Brush Point. It was slow going and I didn't arrive near Brush Point until daylight was breaking.

A WNW wind blows across the end of Brush Point and slightly into the mouth of the Sloughs. As I approached the Point, perhaps a half mile away, I began to notice sizable swells which had to have been caused by waves sweeping the Point and coming into the Sloughs. I also noticed an unusual chop in the water going in the other direction; the flooded Sloughs were beginning to drain back into the Lake, creating an extremely hazardous condition. If I lost power, the current would carry me into the storm on the Lake.

Regardless, I wanted to hunt as close to the Point as possible, so

I crept along hugging the lee shore. It was OK near the shore but just fifty to one hundred yards out were monster waves. With the strong current of the Sloughs heading into the Lake, I knew it would be too risky to hunt where I was so I decided to reverse directions and run farther back up the Sloughs. First though, I couldn't resist a sneak peek at the Lake. I stayed on the protected side near shore, got as close to the Point as I dared, put the bow on the bog and stood up on the seat to take a look at the open Lake. What a sight! I couldn't believe the size of the waves that were sweeping the Point. Even though I was protected, I was frightened. I knew that if I lost power and started drifting, I would be in big trouble. I turned around and motored back up the Sloughs about a half mile, found a decent spot and set my decoys.

Setting the decoys was difficult. The wind was blowing so hard off shore that when I put the motor in neutral to set decoys, I would drift dangerously far out within seconds. Normally I would set anywhere from thirty to sixty decoys, but that day, it was all I could do to set fourteen. Once I got them set, I ran back to shore, put the bow into the bog and dropped the anchor. Because of the wind, I used a miniature blind built by driving two poles in the bog off the transom and tying a piece of canvas between them. By the time I finished it was nearly daylight.

The wind was still strong but I could see occasional patches of clear sky, which would quickly cloud over. What was troubling was that I didn't see any ducks and usually, if the shooting were going to be good, I'd see a few ducks buzzing around at daylight. Suddenly I saw a lone mallard beating against the wind, while working his way along the shoreline toward me. I was determined to get him but just before he got to the blind, he drifted behind me out of range.

While I was turned to watch the mallard, I heard a whir of wings and the unmistakable cooing of bluebills. Sure enough, a bundle of six were sitting in my decoys. When I turned they saw me and took off. I shot and missed with the first barrel but dropped a nice drake with the second. He fell stone-dead and started drifting. I let him go until he got to the edge of the decoys before going after him. Mistake. He drifted so fast that by the time I got to him I was dangerously far from shore and into the swells of the waves sweeping the Point. I got back but it was scary. It was clear that any other ducks I shot would have to be retrieved immediately.

When I got back to the blind, I poured a cup of coffee. Just then a large flock of bluebills flared over the inside edge of the decoys. I picked a nice male and dropped him. Because I went after him right away, I had a little wait while he drifted clear of the decoys. While I waited, I glanced up at the Sloughs. What an incredible sight greeted me. The sky had become overcast again with low hanging greenish-colored clouds. There were hundreds of bundles of ducks dancing over the Sloughs as far as I could see, literally thousands of them. Every duck in Canada and the Dakotas must have migrated. I took a minute to savor the view; it was a sight I'll never forget. Then I picked up the bluebill and headed back to my blind.

After that it was one bundle of ducks after another. I shot only drakes, one at a time. There were mallards, bluebills, ringnecks, redheads and canvasbacks. I had dozens of flocks in the decoys over the course of the morning, some of them had over one hundred ducks. They kept coming, one bunch after another. It was such an amazing sight that I watched them long after I was through shooting.

I stayed until 9:30 a.m., during which time I never saw another hunter. By then I was getting cold and decided to call it a day. I picked up my decoys and made an uneventful trip back.

A couple of other guys hunted later that day. They did OK but it wasn't as good as the early morning. The next day the temperature dropped into the twenties, the Sloughs began to freeze and there wasn't a duck to be found. I didn't hunt that day, or any more that season.

HOW I EARNED AN "A" IN SENIOR ENGLISH

● ●

My friend, Chet, usually exercises sound judgment but the hunting dog he bought in the spring of 1958 was a notable exception.

A short time before the opening of the ruffed grouse season, I happened to stop by his home.

"Pete!" he exclaimed, "Buck has just returned from twenty days of hunting school!"

"You're kidding? You actually paid to send that mutt to school? You must have money you don't know what to do with."

Bristling, he answered, "You'll be surprised at how much he learned. Wait and see."

Buck was a three-year-old, eighty-five pound chocolate Lab. According to Chet, he was a purebred and had papers to prove it, but as far as I was concerned, he was a poorly disguised counterfeit. His neck and shoulders were so large in proportion to the rest of his body that he looked like a cross between a pitbull and a greyhound. He had the manners of a sow, the disposition of a mule and the intelligence of a rock.

Chet, brightening, persisted. "Pete," he said, "remember last year when he wouldn't retrieve no matter how hard I tried to teach him? Since returning from hunting school, he retrieves beautifully."

At the time of this discussion we were standing inside his father's garage. Chet picked up a three-foot length of two by two and threw it out the door as far as he could. Buck, noticing the motion, leaped to his feet and bound after it. Reaching it, he snatched it up in the center and without breaking stride negotiated a one hundred and eighty degree turn and began an even more enthusiastic chase back to where Chet and I were standing just inside the door.

It was a pretty good fetch; however, Buck must not have been paying attention during math class because he ran full blast into the thirty-inch wide door opening with a thirty-six inch long two by two. When he hit the door jam, the sudden deceleration from fifty to zero MPH threatened to drive his rear quarters through his head. Fortunately, the only damage was that he knocked himself out cold. After several minutes of quivering, he awakened sufficiently to make a beeline under the porch. He remained there until evening despite our efforts to coax him out.

I went home convinced that it would take more than hunting school to improve Buck.

The evening before the opening of ruffed grouse season, Chet called me. "Let's go grouse hunting tomorrow."

"Sure," I answered, "pick me up at 6:00 a.m."

"Can I bring Buck?" he asked nervously.

Inwardly I groaned. I didn't want to hunt with Buck, preferring my seasoned dog, Rex, instead but I knew if I refused, Chet would be hurt. "No, I don't mind. Just try to keep him out of trouble."

Thus, the plans were made for an opening day that I'd just as soon forget.

Chet arrived promptly at 6:00 a.m. We put the dogs in the back of the truck and I tried to catch a short nap on the drive to the hunting location.

"Hey, Pete," Chet said, arousing me from my nap. "Are the dogs OK?"

"Huh?" I asked, waking up startled. Then comprehending what he had asked, I answered without looking up, "Yeah, they're OK."

"Come on, Pete, take a look and see what they're doing. You were supposed to keep an eye on the dogs."

"I don't have to look, Chet. What else would a graduate of Duluth Dog School be doing? He's reading the Wall Street Journal."

"Pete! I can't see Buck. I think he may have jumped!"

Buck had a history of jumping from moving pickup trucks; a habit he'd picked up as a youngster. Most dogs catch on after surviving a fall or two, but not Buck. If he saw a bird, rabbit or deer, there was a good chance he'd jump from the pickup to chase after it.

Anticipating beforehand that he might jump, we had tied him on a short leash to the pickup's spare tire. That didn't stop Buck. He jumped anyway. Chet slammed on the brakes and we leaped outside fully expecting to find a dead dog. Fortunately, the leash was tied so short that Buck wasn't able to reach the ground and his bulldog neck saved him from hanging.

"We're going to have to let him ride in the cab. I can't trust him in the pickup box anymore," Chet exclaimed.

Personally, I was all for putting him back in the box and giving him another shot at jumping. Who knows? Perhaps after three or four hundred tries he might figure it out.

"Oh goody!" I said. "I love sharing the front seat with Buck. I enjoy the constant commotion when he's jumping from you to me and on and off the seat. I particularly enjoy the whining and slobbering. Here, let me help him up, poor thing."

I think Buck may have jumped from the back of the truck just to get in the cab. Perhaps he was smarter than I thought. He spent the rest of the trip leering at me and slobbering on my pants while backing up to Chet for attention.

The morning was typical for early October in Wisconsin. The leaves had not yet fallen and the foliage was so thick that you couldn't see more than twenty yards in the woods. The temperature hovered around thirty-five degrees and the brush was dripping with a heavy, wet, cold dew.

"Boy, it sure looks wet out there," Chet said, "maybe we ought to road hunt for a while until it dries up?"

"Naw, don't be such a baby. It's not that wet and it'll dry up shortly." I prevailed and we started to hunt.

Forty-five minutes later we were both soaked to the skin, shivering and headed for hypothermia.

"How far is it back to the truck?" Chet asked.

"I'm not sure," I answered, "but I'm freezing. There's an old deserted pulper's shack just ahead. Why don't we try to find it, build a fire and dry our clothes?"

"Good idea," Chet agreed and we started off to look for the

shack. When we found it, it was apparent that it hadn't been used for a long time as it was nearly falling down.

"We'll never get anything to dry in there," Chet complained. "The windows are out, the walls are a mess and the stove pipe isn't even connected."

"Don't worry about it Chet. We'll figure something out."

Upon close examination the stove seemed to be intact except that the stovepipe wasn't long enough to reach through the ceiling. However, attached to the main building was a six-foot by six-foot tool shed that was in better condition.

We carried the stove into the tool shed and connected the stovepipe, poking the end out the window. Using debris from the pulper's shack for fuel, we built a roaring fire.

"Let's bring in as much wood as possible and stack it in the corner. Then we can get out of these wet clothes and hang them up to dry," I suggested.

Meanwhile, the dogs were standing around looking like a couple of sponges wondering why we had stopped hunting.

"What about the dogs?" Chet asked.

"What do you mean, 'What about the dogs?' They're dogs! They're used to standing around wet. Don't worry about 'em."

It didn't take long before the temperature in the building started to rise. We rapidly removed our clothes and hung them as best we could to dry.

"Let's put some more wood on the fire," I suggested.

"Gee, I dunno Pete, that stove looks pretty hot to me."

"Naw, that's nothing," I answered, opening the door and stuffing as much dry pine in as the stove would hold. "I'll show you how to build a real fire."

In seconds the stove sprang to life and started roaring, crackling and changing color from gray to bright cherry red. The temperature in the building climbed to an astronomical level and both Chet and I backed as far away from the stove as the limited space would allow.

Just then, Chet noticed an old ax handle lying on the floor. Picking it up he said, "Hey Pete, look at this. It must be a million years

OUTDOOR FOLLIES

old . . . YIKES!!!" he screamed as he spotted a huge spider on the underside of the ax handle.

"Throw it out of here!" I yelled.

Chet deftly threw the ax handle out the door. The movement caught the attention of Buck who had been lying down just outside the door. He sprang to his feet and grabbed the ax handle just as it came to rest, turned and charged full steam back to the door of the tool shed.

"NO BUCK! NO!" Chet yelled, but it was too late. All eighty-five pounds of Buck crashed into the interior of the building, sending the stove and the stovepipe crashing to the floor in a shower of flames and sparks.

The next few moments remain clouded in my memory. I dimly remember making a grab for the dog's throat, missing and scorching my thigh in the attempt. Then Chet and I both scrambled for the door at the same time, only to stumble over Buck who was leading the charge for safety. We all went down in a tumble but managed to roll, crawl and jump our way out the door without injury. Once safely outside we watched as the shack and our clothing disappeared in a ball of flames.

"Now what are we going to do?" Chet wailed. "We don't have any clothes and our truck is miles away."

"There's nothing we can do but walk back to the truck, dodging any other hunters we see. It's a good thing we left our guns outside and our boots and hats on while our clothes were drying."

We started carefully sneaking back toward the truck. We hadn't paid much attention to the cover while we were hunting before, but now it seemed that wherever we walked we would run into brambles, thorns and blackberry patches. The dogs thought they were still hunting but there wasn't much we could do except try to keep them as close to us as possible.

"Jeez, Pete, I'm getting scratched to death by this brush, can't we find a better route?"

"There isn't a better route. We'll just have to do the best we can."

Slowly and carefully we worked our way back toward the truck when suddenly, in the direction we needed to walk, I noticed movement. "Chet!" I hissed. "There's somebody in front of us."

We held the dogs alongside of us and watched. I saw flashes of movement. Whoever it was seemed to be working their way toward us. Finally, I got a good look and I nearly fainted. Not thirty yards in front of us, picking early fall mushrooms, were Miss Luella and Miss Tuula Maki, spinster sisters who taught twelfth-grade English at our local high school.

Far from being weak old ladies, this pair had a reputation for immediate and fierce action should any infraction occur in their classroom. For example, when our high school star football player, Hank Fulton, played a little prank on Miss Luella, he was body slammed, put in a head lock and dragged stunned and speechless to the principal's office. You did not mess with the Maki sisters! Behind their backs, the kids called them the "Iron Maidens."

"It's the Iron Maidens," I said. "Quick, turn right and we'll try and sneak around them."

"If they see us like this we're dead," Chet said.

"Tell me about it, get going!"

We started moving to our right attempting to maneuver around them. We made good headway but Buck, alerted that something was up but unable to see above the brush, kept looking in the direction where the sisters were picking mushrooms.

We had one little six-foot clearing to cross during which we would be visible if they happened to look in our direction. We waited until their backs were turned and then attempted to sprint across the clearing. That's when Buck spotted their cat. I couldn't believe it; they had brought their cat with them on a short leash!

Buck took off in a flash after the cat. The cat, a large and ornery-looking male named "Tommy," spotted the dog, let out a howl and broke free from its leash. Tommy then dove into a blackberry bramble and climbed a skinny tree to a crotch about six feet off the ground, where he sat hissing and growling, daring the dog to come close.

Chet, acting involuntarily, yelled, "Buck! Stop! Stop!"

At that the sisters spotted us. "You!" Tuula screeched. "Get over here and get that mangy cur away from my cat before I go to my car and get my shotgun."

"He won't hurt your cat, he can't climb the tree."

"It's not my cat I'm worried about, it's that thing you call a dog. If Tommy takes a notion to jump, that dog is going to spend the next week with a vet wondering where his face went! Now get over there and get him!"

"I . . . I . . . d-d-don't have any clothes on," Chet stammered, trying to hide behind his hat.

"Good grief, I can see what you don't have on, you nitwit. Right now I don't care. Right now I want you to get that dog away from my cat!"

"OK, OK, I'll get him," Chet said, attempting to walk sideways to present only a side view to the teachers.

"Quit walking sideways like a snake and get moving! Yours isn't the first skinny butt I've ever seen. I work summers at the hospital you know. Now hurry up over there and get that dog before Tommy decides to get feisty!"

"Who's that other guy with you?" Luella asked. "I suppose it's that moron friend of yours, Pete?"

She knew me well from school and froze me with a glare. "Peter! You stay right where you are until we get to the bottom of this. And wipe that smirk off your face!"

Meanwhile, Buck was going bananas, jumping and barking up a storm under the tree while the cat leaned toward him hissing and growling.

"Here," Tuula said, "take this leash and put it on that cur and get him away from the tree."

Chet, scratched and bleeding, finally managed to leash Buck and get him away from the tree. He then turned to coax the cat down. That's when Tommy decided to use Chet as a route to the ground. He was on and off Chet in a flash but not before sinking his claws in Chet's leg to keep from slipping as he ran for the safety of Tuula's arms.

"OW!!" Chet screeched.

"Oh quit your whining, you big baby, it's just a scratch," Tuula answered, scooping up Tommy. "Poor baby, are you OK, Tommy? Did that big dog scare you?"

After the cat was calmed down Luella looked at us and said, "What the heck have you two been up to? Where are your clothes?"

Once they heard our story and remembered seeing smoke from the burning building everything made sense.

Not one to miss a golden opportunity, Miss Luella said, "Well boys, I'd bet you'd pay a pretty penny to keep this story off the street?"

"What do you mean?" I said.

"What I mean, Einstein, is that either you and Chet get A's or B's in my senior English class or this story will be spread all over the school. Understand?"

"Err . . . yeah, I got it."

"Now, get to your truck and let us get back to picking mushrooms."

"Ummm, Pete, I just remembered something," Chet said.

"What?"

"My truck keys were in my pants when they burned."

That's how we ended up naked in the back seat of the Iron Maiden's car heading to town to get a second set of keys.

On the way, the local deputy sheriff, Will Ketchum, passed us on the other lane. He stopped, turned and followed us flashing his lights.

Tuula looked at Luella and said, "I guess we should have had that taillight fixed this morning."

The deputy, familiar to all of us, walked up to the driver's window and nearly flipped when he glanced in the back seat and saw Chet and me with our hats in our laps.

The deputy looked at Tuula and said, "Well, well, planning a little party?"

"Don't smart talk me, Will Ketchum!" Tuula snapped. "You're not such a big shot these days that I can't still take you down a peg or two!"

"Yes, Ma'am, I believe you can. Regardless, would you please explain what's going on?"

OUTDOOR FOLLIES

"Yes, I will," retorted Tuula, "but first I'd like to remind you about a little incident that happened two years ago when I chaperoned the prom. Your date was the sheriff's daughter. You may recall me following you out the back door of the gym and catching you in the car with her? Good thing I did too! I kept that little incident to myself the last couple of years but if a word of this gets out, I promise you, I'll be giving the sheriff a call. I don't think that would help your career in law enforcement. Get it?"

Sheriff "Big Cat" Johnson was six foot four and weighed two hundred and forty pounds, not an ounce of it fat and he had a notorious temper. He was also extremely protective of his only daughter.

"No, Ma'am, I don't think it would help my career any. Regardless, I need to know what's going on. I can assure you that if no laws have been broken, nobody will ever hear of this."

"Well," Tuula said. "It's quite a story . . ."

And that's how I got an "A" in English my senior year.

MY THREE LIVES

•••••••••••••••••••

Over a lifetime of outdoor activity, I've had a number of close calls. Here are three of those stories. They are true.

Peter F. Crowley

THE TREE
•••••••

Several weeks before the 1975 deer season I scouted an area, found a nice spruce that I could climb and constructed a stand in it.

Back then, hunting from a tree was a relatively new idea. We built our tree stands in spruce trees that had an abundance of limbs. First, we would remove only enough limbs to provide climbing space. These limbs were cut off a few inches from the trunk which left a "step" for climbing. Once we reached the desired height, we selected two strong limbs that grew out from the tree at the same level but were about eight to twelve inches apart. These two limbs would form a "seat." We would sit facing the tree with one buttock supported on each limb. To be comfortable and improve visibility, we broke off a number of outer limbs and placed them crossways over the limbs on which we sat. Our feet rested on lower limbs. Although primitive by today's standards, these stands were easy to build and quite comfortable.

I liked to be at least thirty feet high so my scent would drift above any approaching deer. After building this particular stand, I measured the height with a rope and found that I was thirty-two feet from the ground. I tested the stand for strength by tying myself to a limb, holding on tight and bouncing on the seat. It seemed fine. I descended the tree, planning to climb it again on opening morning.

The day before the opener we had an unusually severe early season snowstorm, which dropped twenty-five inches of heavy wet snow. On opening morning, because of the snow, driving was difficult but I managed to grind my way along with my four-wheel-drive pickup truck to the spot where I wanted to park. It was several hours before daylight when I arrived but I'd left early because I knew walking would be difficult and slow.

When I reached my tree, I was a little concerned about climbing it, as the limbs were all covered with snow and were slippery. I also noticed that the limbs that hadn't been cut, were heavily weighted with wet snow. I decided to climb the tree anyway but to be very, very careful.

The climb wasn't as difficult as I thought. I got to the seat, brushed the snow off and sat down. The limbs on which I was seated had a heavy snow load on their ends, but spruce limbs are very strong and I was sure they would hold me without any problem. To make certain, I bounced a little on the seat while holding on to other limbs. Everything seemed OK.

I had climbed the tree with my gun slung over my left shoulder. Because the stands are designed to sit facing the tree, it's natural to lean toward the trunk when watching for deer, however; to unsling my rifle, I had to lean slightly backwards. The first thing I should have done was to tie myself in with a safety rope but I decided to remove my rifle from my shoulder first. To do so I reached over with my right hand to take the rifle from my left shoulder, and at that precise instant I heard a loud "crack." Incredibly, both limbs that I was sitting on broke at the same time.

Because I had been leaning slightly backwards when the limbs broke, I fell backwards headfirst with my feet above me. I made an attempt to grab a limb but it was hopeless. Furthermore, my left arm was tangled in the sling. I realized instantly that I would have no chance to survive if I hit headfirst so I tried to straighten my body and land as flat on my back as possible, attempting to distribute the shock over its entire length. Because I had learned to dive when I was growing up on Lake Superior, I was able to get myself turned in the air and managed, except that my butt might have been leading slightly, to hit the ground almost flat on my back. When I hit, all I remember is WHAM!!!

I opened my eyes and was delighted to find myself alive. At the time I didn't think I'd even been knocked out, but later realized I had laid there for over an hour as I had fallen in the dark and now it was full daylight.

When I regained my senses, I tried to stand up but couldn't. I then realized that I had no feeling in my legs. I couldn't move anything from my waist down. "My God," I thought, "I've broken my back and I'm paralyzed!"

I reached for my gun to fire a series of three shots hoping to attract attention, but the sling was still tangled around my arm and the gun barrel was buried deep in the snow and mud below. It was stuck with the butt in the air and buried so deep that I had to turn my upper body on its side and pull as hard as I could in an attempt to free it. It wouldn't budge! I fell back in frustration when suddenly the feeling in my lower body came back. "Thank God," I thought! I got up, pulled my gun out and found the barrel packed with mud. I decided to go home, clean the barrel and return later.

When I got home, my back started hurting so I laid down on the couch. After an hour I couldn't get off the couch because of pain and stiffness. My wife called a physician and he called in a prescription to our local drug store for pain medication. With the medication I was able to function. The doctor didn't suggest I stop in or go to the Emergency Room and since I was able to function after taking the medication, I decided it wasn't necessary.

By using the pain medication, I made it through the season but suffered a lot of back pain. I ended up getting a nice buck (from the ground) but continued to have trouble with my back for nearly a year.

About ten years later I was having some lower back pain and saw a physician. He X-rayed my back and told me that I had arthritis located around an old back fracture. I told him he must have gotten my X-rays mixed up with someone else's, as I had never fractured my back. He said the X-rays were not mixed up and that I had indeed fractured a vertebra in my back at some time in the past. He showed me a hairline fracture, which was still visible on the X-ray. I told him about the fall and we agreed that's when the injury probably occurred

What happened? Spruce limbs are extremely strong but the

heavy, wet snow on the ends of the limbs and my weight were too much. All it took was for me to lean slightly backwards to cause them to snap.

I survived because there was at least eighteen inches of heavy wet snow on the ground to cushion my fall and that I had the presence of mind and ability to turn in the air and land as flat on my back as possible. Why was I initially paralyzed? I don't know. It may have been the shock of the fall that caused a temporary paralysis, or, when I threw myself back in disgust after not being able to pull my gun out, I may have realigned something which had been knocked off center by the fall. Who knows . . .? What I do know is that I was very lucky.

THE BOAT
• • • • • •

In 1985, a few weeks before the ice went out on Lake Superior's Chequamegon Bay, I bought a new fourteen-foot boat with a twenty-five horsepower motor. I was anxious to try it out, hence, the day after the ice went out, I launched my new rig for the first time.

The day was cold and gray with a light north wind. Because of the weather I was dressed in long underwear, woolen pants, woolen shirt, felt-lined boots and a heavy jacket. Since the ice had just gone out, the water temperature was barely above freezing.

I launched my new boat at a boat ramp a short distance from Ashland and motored east toward a place called the Kakagon Sloughs. This area, part of the Bad River Indian Reservation, is remote, and because it was early in the season there were no other boats in the area.

My boat, a stern drive with a tiller, ran fast and smooth. Everything seemed fine when suddenly the tiller slipped from my grasp. I may have hit an underwater deadhead but I'm not certain. Regardless, the result was catastrophic! The boat turned ninety degrees to the left at full speed. Because of the extreme force of the turn I was instantly thrown from the boat. I hit the surface hard, slamming water into my nose and mouth. I fought my way to the surface choking and gagging thinking, "I'm in real trouble, this is one accident

OUTDOOR FOLLIES

I'm not going to survive."

The first thought I had, even before I surfaced, was that since the boat was turning sharply to the left when I was ejected, it would continue to turn in a circle and hit me when I came up. I came to the surface expecting to get hit by a fast-moving boat but found that the boat had slowed to an idle. It was in gear, moving along at two to three MPH, already a couple hundred yards away. Apparently the throttle on the tiller was spring loaded and when I'd let go it remained in gear but slowed to idle speed.

I don't remember the water being cold but it had to be near freezing. I only remember thinking that because of all my heavy clothing and boots I would be pulled down and drown. At first I didn't think I would be able to swim but was amazed to find that although I was a little lower in the water than usual, I could. I had always been a strong swimmer, having grown up on Lake Superior, and when I saw the shore about a half-mile away, I figured with a little luck I should be able to reach it.

As I started swimming toward shore, I took one more look for the boat and noticed that it was turning in a large circle. I watched it for a while and realized that if it continued to circle, it would eventually pass near me. I decided to try to position myself so I could grab it as it passed me. When it came by, I tried to grab it but missed by a couple of feet. Frantically, I swam after it as hard as I could, coming close to panic but after a short chase I realized it was hopeless. I would have to wait for another pass. Sure enough, the boat started making another big circle. This time I positioned myself so that the boat would hit me if I didn't grab it. As it came by I grabbed the bow, but because of the combination of the pull from the forward motion of the boat and the weight of my soaked clothing, I didn't have the strength to pull myself in. I worked my way toward the middle of the boat, where it would be easier to get over the side, and made another attempt but failed. I just didn't have the strength! Not knowing what else to do, I hung onto the boat hoping another boater would come by. After a while I started getting exhausted. Realizing that another boater wasn't likely to come by, I decided to make another attempt to get in. This time I put every ounce of strength I could muster into the effort, more than I thought I had, and just barely managed to inch my stomach over the side a bit at a time until I fell, totally spent, into the boat.

That's the end of the story. Once again I had survived a dicey situation. I motored back to the landing, loaded my boat on my trailer and headed home. I never really felt cold during the ordeal, but by the time I got home I was shivering uncontrollably. I went directly into a hot bath and a couple hours later went to work.

THE ICE
・・・・・

Over the years I've had a number of close calls while ice fishing on Lake Superior. I fell through twice, had to row back a time or two when the wind blew the ice out, and needed to use my compass more than once to get back during a surprise snowstorm.

Once, when I fell through as a youngster while fishing with my dad, I can hardly remember being in the water because I was back on the ice so fast. When the ice blew out, we had a boat with us and rowed back without incident. During the snowstorm we used a compass to find our way back.

Any of these incidents could have been very bad but were not. However, there was one more event that was bad. Here's that story.

It happened on a Saturday morning in early spring. Because the weather had been particularly warm for early spring, I called Norm, my fishing partner, late on the previous Friday afternoon to discuss whether or not the ice was still solid enough to try lake trout fishing the next day. He told me that his dad and a couple of other guys had been out that very day and had drilled several holes on the way home. They told Norm that the ice was still thirty inches thick and had not deteriorated too much in the warm weather. They also reported that they had made a nice catch of trout. Norm and I decided to fish with them on Saturday at the same location.

Saturday began with a beautiful spring morning. It was clear and calm with the temperature already above freezing.

We planned to fish near Long Island, which was about a seven-mile run from where we unloaded our snowmobiles. We packed our gear on our sleds and started. There were six of us in the group, Norm and I, his dad and three friends of his dad. We each had our own snowmobile and sled. Norm and I knew the route and started out leading the group across the ice. The ice looked bad so I stopped a couple of times thinking I should test it with my ice bar, but had packed the ice bar under all my other gear and was reluctant to unpack the entire sled to get it out.

On the way out, I dropped into a couple of slush holes; but it had been a year when there were a lot of slush pockets on the ice and I thought they were just some old slush holes that had gotten soft on top but were still frozen underneath.

As we were cruising along, I noticed a fish frozen beneath the surface of the ice. I was curious about what kind of fish it was and how it had gotten trapped in the ice so I circled back to get a better look. Meanwhile, the rest of the group continued on toward Long Island, except Norm, who was just behind me. As I slowed down, the back of my machine dropped deep into another slush pocket and stayed in it for six to eight feet. I gunned the machine to pull out and stopped when the machine stayed on top of the ice. I told Norm, who had stopped next to me, that I was really getting nervous and was going to check the ice. I got my ice bar out and poked into the slush hole. It was nothing but slush on top of the water, I had gone completely through!

I looked at Norm in astonishment and exclaimed, "I went through . . . this ice is rotten; we have to stop the other guys before somebody drowns!" As I said it, I looked in the direction of the rest of the group and my blood ran cold! They were stopped, standing in a huddle, but one snow machine and rider was missing. I looked at Norm and said, "Somebody went through!" He glanced at the group huddled together and said, "It's my dad!"

I said, "It isn't your dad, I recognize his sled on the ice. It's somebody else. We better go slow and careful before somebody else goes through!" I might as well have talked to the wind. One thing about Norm, he formed his own opinions, acted fast and did what he felt he needed to do. Without any hesitation he started his machine and headed toward the group at full speed without regard for his own safety. I followed, but at a slower pace picking and choosing a route that seemed safe.

While I worked my way toward the rest of the group I had a sick feeling that whoever went through was lost forever. He had already been underwater for a long time and there was no sign of him. It was horrible to contemplate what he must have been going through at that moment. I didn't think there was any hope of getting him out. The best we could hope for was to avoid losing someone else.

As I approached the group, I noticed that they were throwing a rope with a two-foot piece of ax handle attached to it out toward a slush hole where I presumed the machine had disappeared. As I got closer, I looked at the hole and it appeared that there was a hat floating on the water. As I got closer yet, I saw that the hat was on Ralph, the guy who had gone through. He hadn't drowned after all. His entire body was submerged up to his mouth and he was hanging on with his fingertips to some very fragile candled ice. He looked terrified and appeared as though he was just about to slip under.

The ice on which he went through was much more rotten than the ice we were on. Because he went through so far out in front of the other guys, they were able to stop on the relatively safe ice. They were now trying to throw the ax handle to Ralph, but the rope wasn't nearly long enough to reach him.

I saw all of this as I was approaching the group. Meanwhile, Norm, who had already been there for several minutes, sized up the situation and realized that the other guys, who were all seventy plus years old, were probably not going to be able to get Ralph out. Norm removed his canvas teepee from his sled and partially opened it. He planned to use it if he broke through, hoping the flat teepee would spread out over enough ice to support him. Then he got the rope and ax handle from the other guys. He tucked the rope and ax handle under one arm, the shelter under the other, and ran out to a point where he was able to reach Ralph with the rope. As he ran, he broke through the ice up to his knees three times but was able to throw himself on the teepee and get out.

When he got close enough, he started throwing the rope to Ralph but Ralph was afraid to let go of the ice to grab it.

OUTDOOR FOLLIES

Meanwhile, I started to work my way out to Norm to help get Ralph out. I took off all my outer clothing thinking that if I went through I might be able to get myself out if I wasn't burdened with heavy clothing. I decided that rather than trying to use a teepee like Norm did, I would use my ice bar to check the ice in front of me and try to find a relatively safe route. I could see where there had been an old snowdrift under which the ice was still pretty solid and I was able to pick my way to a point about six feet to the left of Norm.

Norm was still throwing the ax handle to Ralph and Ralph was still refusing to make a grab for it. Ralph never said a word the entire time but he looked terrified. After I got there Norm and I started yelling at him to grab the stick but he was afraid to do so. Finally, Norm made a perfect toss nearly hitting Ralph on the head. The ax handle fell about a foot in front of Ralph, who looked at it for the longest time and finally, with our strong encouragement, made a grab for it. There was a little slack in the line and when Ralph grabbed the ax handle he went completely under. Norm took up the slack in the rope and pulled Ralph to the surface. He attempted to pull him up on the ice, but the ice was so rotten it kept breaking in front of Ralph. Therefore, Norm slowly pulled Ralph through the ice toward us.

Meanwhile, I was standing alongside doing nothing but watching the action. During this time I took a couple of seconds to glance around. The ice was black and filled with water. The old snowdrift on which I was standing was solid compared to the rest of the ice but every step I took caused water to "jump" in the ice all the way around me. It was amazing we were able to stand on it at all.

By now Norm had pulled Ralph through the ice almost to him. It looked to me as though one more pull would position Ralph right next to Norm and cause him to also fall in. I yelled, "Don't pull him any closer, you'll both be in. Hand the rope to me and I'll keep tension on him until you can get over to this old snowbank where the ice is better." Norm gave me that "I'll do what I want to do look," and for a second I was certain he'd give another pull, but he didn't. He handed the rope to me, picked up his teepee and took one step backwards and fell through. Fortunately, he was able to throw his upper body on the tent and crawl out and slowly work his way to the snowdrift.

Once we were together, we kept the tension on the rope and let it out slowly as we worked our way back toward better ice. When we were situated on better ice, we again started pulling Ralph but still were only able to pull him through the ice instead of up on top of it. Finally, after we backed up farther yet, we were able to pull him up on to the ice. As soon as he got on the solid ice, he tried to stand up. We yelled "NO!" But it was too late. He went through, completely disappearing under the water and ice. I thought we might have lost him forever, as all I could see was the rope going into the broken ice. We started pulling and thankfully Ralph broke through to the surface hanging on to the ax handle for dear life. He was a sight to behold . . . his eyes were as big as saucers and he had ice crystals hanging from his hair and clothing. Thank God he had the presence of mind to hang onto the ax handle when he went under. This time we instructed him not to get up, that we would pull him over the ice to the snow machines. He complied.

When we got to the snow machines, Ralph let go of the rope and gingerly stood up. He was visibly shaken by the ordeal and on the verge of hypothermia. The rest of the group were also badly frightened and simply wanted to get back home. We still had to cross over bad ice to return home and I suggested we travel single file and carefully pick our way. I guess it wasn't my day for suggestions because after we traveled the first fifty yards every machine was on a different vector heading for the landing at full speed, myself included.

Later, we got Ralph's story. After Norm and I had stopped, he was leading the group. He didn't notice the change in ice conditions and ran onto the rotten ice at half throttle. The snowmobile started breaking through so Ralph opened the throttle to full speed hoping to turn and get back onto better ice. Unfortunately, he was only able to turn in a slow semicircle and the snowmobile started sinking. Just before it went under he stood on the seat and jumped onto the ice, spreading his arms and legs hoping it would support him. It didn't. He was dressed in a heavy flight suit and at first it helped keep him buoyant but then slowly started to fill with water. He tried to climb on the ice but it was so rotten that it kept breaking under him. His clothing got heavier and heavier causing him to sink lower and lower into the water. He kept trying to get out but even putting his arms on the ice caused it to collapse into slush. Finally, he felt he only had a few seconds left before going under permanently and decided to hold on by his fingertips. That's where he was when Norm and I first arrived.

Norm was a hero that day. His leadership and fast action without regard for his own life saved Ralph's life.

It was a very scary ordeal. For years afterwards I had nightmares, but could never remember much about them. One morning I remembered what I had been dreaming . . . it was about Ralph going through the ice. Once I remembered the nightmare, I never had it again.

Since then I have a new respect for the ice. I'm nervous even when there's no need to be and I always check the ice conditions myself.

BEAR GREASE

• • • • • • • • • • • • • • • • •

Several years ago my hunting companion, Dave, and I were discussing how we should hunt bear during the upcoming season.

Because I've never been thrilled about the prospect of stumbling through the brush in the heat of early autumn chasing after a pack of dogs, and even the mere mention of raising hounds would have been grounds for divorce, it seemed that we would either have to sneak hunt or use bait.

We live along the shore of Lake Superior, where the brush can be so thick that, in places, you need a compass in your hand with every step. The visibility is like a jungle, especially when the leaves are on the trees. In fact, if you can see thirty yards, it's a long distance. Up here, hunters who are successful sneaking around trying to find a bear are about as common as passenger pigeons, so we decided to use bait.

It's important to have your bait in a remote location, Accordingly, the biggest problem associated with hunting bears with bait is carrying the bait to the hunting location, which is usually at least a mile from the nearest road. I had an idea to solve that problem.

"Dave," I said, "lugging all that bait we hauled into our stands last year was a lot of work."

"What do you mean WE?" he answered. "I did most of the hauling because you were constantly whining about your sore back."

"Very funny. Anyway, I've got a great idea this year, we'll just use my boat . . ." I tried to explain but was rudely interrupted by his rapid departure, which was punctuated by his yelling over his shoulder, "I just remembered, I promised my wife I would weed her flower bed. Besides, I'm still limping from your last great idea."

Encouraged by his enthusiasm I jumped off the porch and followed him saying, "This is a great idea Dave, we'll use my boat to haul the bait. All we have to do is load the boat with bait and find a remote spot along the shore. The only work will be carrying the bait a block or so into the woods."

"Oh yeah," he said, eyeing me suspiciously, "what if the weather is bad? You know how sick I get in rough water. Also, it's risky on Lake Superior in bad weather with that little boat of yours. I don't like rough water, I nearly drowned once already."

"Not a problem. If the weather is bad, we won't go."

At the time I came up with this bright idea, baiting regulations were more liberal than they are now and almost anything could be used for bait. Thinking it would be good bait, I was able to secure six, five-gallon cans of used deep-frying oil that had been discarded by a local Chinese restaurant. The used frying oil, combined with a couple pails of fish guts and two hundred pounds of applesauce I'd cooked up in a fifty-five-gallon drum from early apple windfalls, made up the load of bait for our first trip.

It was a nice warm early autumn day with little or no wind. We loaded the bait in the boat while it was on the trailer. After it was loaded I noticed the trailer springs were flat, even bent backwards a bit. We obviously had a pretty heavy load.

When I looked at all that bait, I wondered if my boat would sink as soon as I launched it, as I had no way of knowing whether or not I'd exceeded the manufacturer's recommended carrying capacity, except that it was a safe bet that we would after Dave and I got in. Who pays attention to carrying capacity anyway? I mean, have you ever heard of anybody who carries a scale around for such a purpose? As far as I was concerned, carrying capacity was one pound less than what would sink the boat.

I held my breath and launched the boat. Other than taking a little water over the transom, it went OK. I pulled it over to the dock and noticed it was riding a little low in the water, so low in fact that I was a little concerned about getting in. When it didn't sink when we got in I took it as a good omen.

I started the motor and we headed to the location where we intended to hunt, stopping about three hundred yards from shore to

OUTDOOR FOLLIES

survey the area. When we found what appeared to be a promising spot, I attempted to restart the motor in order to move in for a closer look.

Unlike most newer motors, my outboard would start in gear as well as in neutral, because several months earlier the part that locks the motor in neutral when starting had malfunctioned and I had removed it. Naturally, I didn't think it was necessary to replace the part. It was just a nuisance . . . one more thing to break.

My motor tended to flood when warm and when I tried to restart it, I couldn't get it going. After several dozen pulls on the starter rope without success I became angry. The more I pulled the madder I got and the more stubborn the motor seemed to become. I glared at Dave, who seemed to be amused at my dilemma. I have a quick temper and flew into a minor rage at my stubborn motor. Enraged, I stood up for additional leverage and gave a vicious pull. Surprisingly, the motor sprang to life, unfortunately with the throttle in the full open position. The boat took off with a roar, spilling Dave, the oil, fish guts and applesauce into the bottom, and me over the transom into the lake.

Dave, who up to this point had been enjoying the spectacle from the front of the boat, was all arms and legs as he frantically tried to scramble through the slippery mixture to gain control of the motor.

There's nothing like a surprise dunk in Lake Superior to cool a hot temper. When I surfaced and saw Dave slipping and sliding on his hands and knees in all that slop, as he was frantically trying to scramble to the back of the boat to get at the motor, I nearly split a gut. It was a hoot. We could have made a million dollars if I had a movie camera. He'd barely get started and he'd fall backwards or sideways, skinning a shin or an elbow in the process. Even above the roar of the motor I could hear him screaming at me . . . my, my such language. I suppose it wasn't polite to laugh, but it was funny. He looked like a monkey on a new pair of ice skates.

Finally, after falling several times and skinning a considerable amount of flesh from both his shins and elbows, Dave was able to gain control and swung by to pick me up.

He was drenched in slop from head to foot, looked as though

he'd been on the losing end of a fight with a wildcat and smelled very, very bad!

He had a maniacal grin on his face and said "I really should let you drown. I mean it . . . I really should."

"You can't, Dave, that would be murder."

"Ha! They'd probably give me a medal."

Reluctantly, he helped me into the boat.

We went to shore and got rid of as much bait as we could. By the time we were finished I was as smelly as Dave, but we were successful in starting a pretty decent bear bait. We couldn't get all the slop out, so we had to leave a little sloshing around in the bottom of the boat. And the smell . . . bad, really bad. That's when I noticed the wind picking up and it wasn't blowing off shore.

"Hey Dave, the wind is picking up, we gotta get out of here."

The sky had turned gray and the wind picked up to gale force, churning the Lake into a mass of whitecaps. Because of the waves, I could only travel at a snail's pace, which meant it would be a couple of hours before we got back to the landing.

In short order, Dave's face started taking on the same gray pallor as the sky. The slop sloshing around in the boat and the stink probably hurried things along, because within a few minutes he was "yakking" everything he had eaten in the last twenty-four hours. "Holy cow," I said, "it's amazing. I would never have believed it was possible for a single human being to barf so many times. I'm going to write this up for one of those medical journals. By the way, would you mind trying to get your head over the side when you throw up? We've got a big enough mess in the boat already."

Dave shot me a malevolent look. "If I survive this, and I don't think I will, I'll never touch this boat again. I must have been out of my mind to agree to this hair-brained scheme."

"Hey, don't get mad at me. I can't help it if you have a weak stomach."

Being sick was bad enough but he also had an absolute phobia about rough water, probably something he picked up as a kid when his older brother tried to teach him to swim by throwing him off the boat dock in six feet of water. Between being sick and afraid, he

OUTDOOR FOLLIES

was a very miserable bear hunter.

I, on the other hand, not troubled by such phobias or seasickness, was entertained by watching cresting six-foot waves threaten to crash down on us from behind, and by listening to creative comments from Dave on some interesting changes he was planning for my anatomy if we ever reached shore. Fortunately, by the time we reached shore, he was so sick that all he wanted to do was get home fast.

I still think using my boat for bear hunting was a good idea, although I never tried it again after that trip. However, with bear season just around the corner it's time to start thinking about this season. Let's see now, if I had twelve bear hounds and they ate five pounds of food per day at a cost of a dollar per pound, what would it cost me to own them? A divorce would probably cost me quite a bit more. Yeah, better forget about the hounds.

CAMP PRANKS

••••••••••••••••

I have a fear of large animals. Large meaning anything over three ounces. All my life animals have tried to bite, kick, chase or stomp me. Once, I even had a mouse try to bite me because I opened a drawer and caught it stealing cereal. Can you believe it? If it would have been anybody else, the mouse would have run, but he took one look at me and decided to fight. You'll argue that old Bowser wouldn't hurt a flea but I've got scars on my butt to prove otherwise. I love animals and have had many pets, but I'm afraid of them. They know it too. Old Bowser may never have hurt a flea in his life but one look at me and he's considering otherwise. Many times I've had some mangy cur run up to me, snarling and growling, looking for all the world as though he's going to rip me to shreds, only to have his owner laugh and say, "Ha, ha, ha, don't worry, he's friendly. He wouldn't hurt a flea." Meanwhile, Mr. Friendly is slinking toward me with his hair on end, growling deep in his throat. Friendly all right . . . friendly as a rattlesnake.

I am particularly afraid of bears. I've never been hurt, or even threatened by a bear but they just plain scare the heck out of me.

Several years ago some friends and I went on a fishing trip. We were flown into a remote lake in northern Ontario and dropped off to spend a week in a tent.

About a month before the trip I received a book in the mail from my friend, Mike, along with a note saying, "Pete, this is a great book. You'll love it." The book, "Alaskan Bear Tales" by Larry Kaniut, is a gruesome series of hair-raising stories of true bear attacks. Reading such a book just before a wilderness fishing trip probably wasn't a good idea but once I started it, I couldn't put it down.

Peter F. Crowley

When we arrived at the camp, we found that the tent the outfitter had set up for us was so full of holes that we couldn't use it. Luckily, I'd brought along a portable screen tent in which we intended to cook, and a small pop-up tent for my personal use. We decided that I'd use the little tent and the other guys would sleep in the screened-in tent.

We set up the tents in the only two flat areas we could find. We kept the food in the outfitter's tent that was adjacent to the screen tent. My tent was thirty yards away, slightly deeper in the brush.

The fishing was fabulous and so was the weather. Everything went fine for the first couple of days.

Regardless, I was concerned about bears. I was alone in that little tent and because it's illegal to bring a firearm or pepper spray into Canada, I felt vulnerable. If a bear really wanted to grab me, there wasn't much I could do about it, as all I had for protection was my hatchet.

The first few nights passed uneventfully. Then Mike mentioned one morning that he'd heard a large animal near the camp during the night. I looked all around in the daylight but didn't see any sign of bears, nonetheless I was on edge.

We turned in when the sun went down and spent a half hour or so shooting the breeze. The other guys knew about my bear fear and teased me about it but I refused to let it bother me. Eventually, everybody fell asleep except me. I was uneasy and kept thinking that I was hearing sounds outside the tent. Twice, I opened the flap and looked around with my flashlight but didn't see anything. Finally, I drifted off to sleep. Then I did hear something! We had stored some empty pop cans between the tents and some animal was digging through them.

I yelled to the other guys, "Did you hear that?"

Mike answered sleepily, "No, I was sleeping. I didn't hear anything."

I opened the tent flap and looked toward the pop cans. I didn't see anything, but there was some brush between my tent and the pop cans through which I couldn't see, so I asked the other guys to shine a light into that brush. They did, and assured me there were no

OUTDOOR FOLLIES

animals around. That's when the thought hit me. Were they pulling a little prank on me?

I warned them by saying, "You guys better not be screwing around." They laughed and accused me of being paranoid.

I lay in the tent a long time listening, but didn't hear any other noise. Eventually, I fell asleep. I must have been asleep for several hours when suddenly I was awakened by some noise. I listened intently. Something was definitely at the pop cans! It couldn't be the other guys because it was the middle of the night and they would have been asleep for hours. It must be some small animal I thought. Then I heard it again, closer, and it didn't sound small; it sounded large and was headed my way! I was on the edge of panic. I grabbed my hatchet and waited. Nothing. Then I heard it again, louder. I got out of my sleeping bag just as I heard a claw rip across the back of my nylon tent. "There's a bear out there!" I screamed!

Mike woke up and flashed his light around. "I don't see anything Pete. Are you sure you heard something?"

"Heard something?" I screeched! "He practically tore my tent open. I'm getting out of here and moving into the screened tent with you guys." I grabbed my sleeping bag, hatchet and flashlight and opened my tent flap. As I started walking toward the other tent, I flashed my light to the rear of my tent looking for a bear and then I saw it. A thin piece of monofilament fishing line. The line was tied to a cut limb in such a way that when it was pulled, the limb would scratch deeply across the back of my tent. A second line was attached to several pop cans and both lines headed back toward their screened-in tent.

"You dirty rats are going to pay! I hope you didn't think I fell for your childish prank. I only played along until I figured out what you were doing. You can rest assured, I'll get even!"

Howls of laughter emanated from their tent. It would start to quiet down and then they'd start laughing again. I'd been so badly frightened and I was so relieved that it wasn't a bear that I wasn't angry. That would come later. It was a good trick. I had to admit it. They finally shut-up and went to sleep as I lay in my sleeping bag with evil thoughts running through my mind. Mike was the ringleader, no doubt about that. The other guys went along but they never would have thought up such an elaborate plan. I didn't know how, or when, but I'd get even.

This trick was supposed to be in retaliation for a silly little prank that I'd pulled on a previous trip. Any little prank I might have played was nothing compared with what they did to me. It was like dropping an atomic bomb in retaliation for a firecracker. This was war and I intended to get even one by one.

The first thing I needed to do was call a truce.

"OK," I agreed the next morning, "it was a good trick. Ha, ha, ha. I suppose I've pulled a few minor pranks in the past. Tell you what, let's all have one more good laugh and then we'll forget about it and any other pranks on this trip and concentrate on fishing." They agreed and everybody had a good final laugh and forgot about it . . . everybody except me that is.

I spent months thinking about revenge. What should I do? Mike is pretty clever so I'll have to be careful with him.

By sheer circumstances, almost a year later, Bill became my first victim.

Bill spends a lot of time in the outdoors guiding bear hunters, hunting ducks and bow hunting for deer. I won't go into detail, but Bill got a citation from a Wisconsin conservation warden having to do with a fisher. It was a minor violation and Bill paid the fine and that was the end of it, except, just as the warden left, he said, "Bill, you know fishers are managed by the Federal government and I will have to inform them of this incident. I doubt if they'd be interested since we've already prosecuted on a state level but it is a Federal violation and they might contact you."

Federal penalties are severe. You can be thrown in prison for stepping on a protected bug. Bill was worried sick about it. Would they come after him? Could he lose his guide license? Then he made a big mistake. He told me about it.

Months went by without hearing anything and Bill eventually forgot about it . . . but I didn't. I waited until April 1st, six months later, and figured it was about time Bill heard from the Feds.

My plan was to send him a registered letter from the Federal court in Milwaukee informing him he was to appear in court on such and such a day. He would be informed that he was going to be charged with section such and such, a violation that was punishable by a fine of up to $100,000 and ten years in jail. The letter would suggest he should hire an attorney.

I was afraid to actually mail him the letter. Bill might go ballistic and run to some Federal agent with the letter. I thought they might take a rather dim view of my using the postal service for a prank. Also, I didn't want to leave Bill hanging too long and give him a heart attack. Therefore, I decided to ask his wife, Judy, to help me. She loved the idea and was only too happy to assist.

I remember seeing registered mail stickers in the lobby of the post office. All I had to do was pick one up and put it on the envelope. He'd never notice it actually hadn't been run through the post office. The sticker even had some sort of serial number. It was perfect, especially when his wife "signed" for it. Next I needed an envelope. With the new photocopying equipment I had at my office, that was easy. I simply copied an eagle and a fake address to a blank envelope. It looked perfect, just like real stationery.

Unfortunately, I couldn't be there when he opened the letter or almost certainly he'd catch on. I gave the letter to Judy and she handed it to Bill when he came home from work. I planned to arrive about a half hour later. Judy told me later that Bill read the letter and turned white. He was stunned. He read it again and again. He hadn't told Judy about the possible Federal involvement on the fisher incident and when she asked him what the letter was about, he played dumb, "Oh it's nothing, nothing Dear, don't worry about it." Then he took the letter and sat on the stairs reading it over and over again. About that time I showed up. Judy was tied up in knots to keep from laughing and she finally spilled the beans. He had been had, on April 1st no less. He fell for it, hook, line and sinker. He was so relieved that he wasn't angry. He claimed he hadn't been one hundred percent fooled but Judy and I knew better.

Revenge is sweet, fun even, and I found I was looking forward to my next victim. There were only two guys left, Jerry and Mike. Jerry really wasn't involved in the planning of the bear incident, although he had a good laugh at my expense, reason enough for severe retaliation; but he wasn't the guy I was really after. Also, he doesn't have an evil mind and he'd be too easy to fool. No real challenge for the likes of me. No, I wanted bigger game. I decided to let Jerry off the hook. Mike was the ringleader, the planner. He was the guy I wanted and it would be easier to get him if I forgot about Jerry and went underground for a while.

I didn't know what to do. Mike lived in a different city and wasn't aware of Bill's fake letter to appear in court. Perhaps a letter from the IRS was in order, something about an audit? I decided against that plan because he probably didn't cheat on his taxes anyway, and was so precise on his returns he'd probably welcome an audit. I mulled it over for months but couldn't come up with much. Thinking about various ideas reminded me of a great trick my uncle had once told me about and I wondered if I could pull that trick off on Mike.

It happened years ago at the local paper mill. There was an employee who worked the evening shift stoking the coal fires that provided steam for the mill. It was known that this person had a great fear of bears, just like me. If you were afraid of bears, loading the coal bin was not a place you wanted to be during the night shift because the coal shed was located near the woods by the lakeshore, and in those early days there often were bears roaming the lakeshore.

It so happened that the local hardware store had an old stuffed grizzly bear that had deteriorated and the owner was about to throw it out. My uncle happened to be there and asked if he could have the head. "Sure," the owner replied. My uncle cut the head off and took it to the paper mill that evening. After sneaking through the brush to the coal shed he hid and waited. The coal passer was shoveling coal from the coal shed to a chute that carried the coal to the paper mill basement floor near the boiler. The weather was hot and the door to the coal shed was open. My uncle peeked in and watched the coal passer shoveling coal. He'd pick up a shovelful, walk several feet to the chute and shovel it in. Just as he picked up a shovelful of coal, my uncle scratched on the door frame. When the coal passer looked up, my uncle poked the grizzly's head through the door. The coal

OUTDOOR FOLLIES

passer froze! He stared in disbelief! Here was a huge bear just a few feet away. His eyes grew large and he looked terrified. He kept the coal on the shovel between himself and the bear and slowly walked backwards toward the chute, but instead of shoveling the coal into the chute, he jumped into it.

It was a great prank and has merit but Mike isn't afraid of bears. I needed something else.

Shortly thereafter, I was talking to a friend who was also a friend of Mike. I don't know how we got on the subject but he mentioned that Mike was terrified of snakes, a pathological fear. "Really," I said, "no kidding."

I spent months searching for just the right snake. I finally settled on a rubber snake that looked more like a snake than a snake did. I bought several of them. I didn't know exactly how I was going to use them but I'd figure something out.

That summer we planned a fishing trip to Lac Seul, a huge lake in northern Ontario. I brought the snakes along thinking I would put them in his sleeping bag or something along that line.

The camp was a series of remote cabins. Our group occupied one cabin and other people occupied the other cabins. There was one shower facility for the entire group consisting of a building with four showers, two for men and two for women.

When I used the shower, I noticed there was a vent from the stall through the ceiling. The vent extended into the stall and ended about eighteen inches above the soap dish. While I was showering the plan came to me. I would climb on the roof and drop a snake down the vent while Mike was in the shower. If he was as afraid of snakes as I was led to believe, dropping a snake into his shower stall should prove interesting.

This little prank alone wasn't enough to exact the level of revenge I was looking for and it wouldn't be all that funny if I were the only person to witness it. So I decided to spice things up by inviting as many people to the party as I could. There were plenty of other fishermen from the other cabins who thought it was a great idea and agreed to show up. I even invited the camp caretaker and his girlfriend who were only too happy to participate. I explained that Mike was a big prankster and I was planning a little prank to get even. I told them he was terrified of snakes and that I intended to drop a snake into his shower stall while he was showering. Then, when he exited the stall, as I hoped he would, he would find other snakes on the dressing area floor and on his clothing, strategically located to guide him out the door naked, only to find himself the butt of a great joke and hear the laughter of all the spectators.

Everything had to be perfect. I couldn't do a thing to let on. I didn't even tell anybody until the last minute. Everybody was catching fish and we were several days into the trip. Mike was off his guard. Every evening we all showered after fishing and Mike almost always would shower last. Earlier, while Mike was fishing, I made a practice run. I climbed on the roof and dropped a snake down the vent a couple of times and it worked perfectly. Plop . . . right into the shower stall. The snakes looked even more natural when wet.

Finally the big day arrived. We all finished showering and as usual, Mike headed to the shower last. Everybody was already alerted and as soon as Mike entered the shower building, people started heading in that direction. I warned them to not make too much noise. They were to stroll casually toward the shower building.

I sneaked into the building and listened. Mike was in the shower and the water was running. I had to act fast. I placed the snakes on the floor, carefully giving him just enough room to run between them to the door. Then I quickly climbed a ladder to the roof and tip-toed over to the vent. Everything was perfect, the water was running and Mike was enjoying his shower. Then I dropped the snake. I found out later it landed right in the soap dish. Instead of the howl I expected there was only a terrified squeal, then I heard a yowl. "SNAKE!" he yelled and ran out the shower stall only to find himself surrounded by snakes with the only apparent escape route out the door. "YIKES! Snakes! Snakes! It's full of snakes in here!" he screamed as he fled the building into the bright sunshine. A chorus of laughter greeted him. It sounded like a thousand people instead of a dozen or so. "Hey Mike," I yelled from on top of the building, "give me a nice smile for this video camera."

OUTDOOR FOLLIES

It's been over now for several years. We've decided to declare a truce. We've actually made a few fishing trips without an incident. Yet, I still sleep with one eye open and am continuously on the lookout for a good prank . . . you never know when it might come in handy.

ADVENTURES WITH FOOD

INTRODUCTION TO OUTDOOR COOKING

I was seven or eight years old when I was first introduced to an outdoor meal. My parents were out for the evening and my older sisters decided to cook supper over an outdoor fire in the backyard. We didn't own a dog, so they used me to test their culinary skills. I was suspicious because I'd only recently recovered from a broken arm suffered the previous year as a result of one of their schemes.

It happened after I overheard them discussing whether or not I could ride my rocking horse on top of a six foot long by eight inch wide basement railing as an act in a circus they were planning. After talking it over, they decided it was a bad idea and dropped it but I had the idea in my head and was obsessed with it. I was certain I could do it and told them so. They warned me not to, but when their backs were turned I tried it anyway. I fell six feet to the basement floor. They considered themselves blameless but I considered the accident their fault; they shouldn't have put such a crazy idea in my head in the first place.

"Peter," she said, "try one of these potatoes I cooked in the fire."

The fire wasn't a fire. It was what my dad called a "white man's fire," which meant it was a smoky smudge. The potato, which she had extracted with a stick from the smudge, looked like a lump of coal. The smudge smelled like smoldering garbage at the dump. I picked up the potato and burned my fingers. Dropping the potato in pain, I started crying. It was not to my credit that they were able to quiet me down and convince me to try it again.

After it cooled, I peeled off some of the charred exterior and took a tentative bite. It was burned on the outside and raw on the inside. I spit it out.

"What did it taste like?" she asked.

"I'd tell you what it tasted like but you'd tell Ma what I said and I'd get my mouth washed out with soap," I answered.

The next two entrees of burned wieners and beans with ashes were not a whole lot better. As far as I was concerned, camp cooking left a lot to be desired and other than a few rare exceptions, I haven't really changed my opinion.

NEVER FORGET A TOOTHBRUSH

As I grew older and started camping, I had to learn to do my own outdoor cooking. I wasn't very successful and my meals were about as tasty as my sister's. On one of these camping trips, I witnessed an amusing incident. It didn't directly involve camp food but did serve as an example of why it's always a good idea to have a toothbrush handy when trying new appetizers.

I was about ten or eleven at the time. Two friends and I were camping alongside the Johnson pasture just above the White River. Our plan was to hike in, set up our tent, stay overnight and get up early the next morning for the opening of trout season.

We had plenty of good food. My mother had packed hamburger patties, canned beans and marshmallows. She'd also packed my toothbrush and toothpaste in the food sack to remind me to brush my teeth after I ate.

After setting up the tent, my two friends, Billy and Richard, suggested that we take a hike down to look at the river. I agreed and off we went.

On the way to the river we crossed through Johnson's pasture, which was amply dimpled with fresh cow pies. Boys being boys, we started throwing rocks into the cow pies. Pretty soon it became a game; who could toss the biggest rock?

Billy had just tossed a softball-sized rock with a nifty throw directly into a cow pie and splattered its contents a good four or five feet. Richard, not to be outdone, picked up a large flat rock that he was barely able to lift. Most of the previous rock throwing had caused a little splattering but so far we had managed to remain pretty clean, however, the rock Richard picked up looked like it could do some serious damage so I backed up. Billy, who was off to one side, seemed mesmerized. He stared with his mouth open as he watched Richard lift the huge flat rock. Struggling, Richard got the rock over his head and made a perfect drop directly on top of a mammoth cow pie.

It was as though a land mine had gone off. An unbelievable explosion of cow manure. I mean, the stuff was flying! I was far enough away to avoid being hit and Richard was saved by the low trajectory, but Billy wasn't so lucky. Incredibly, Richard scored a hole in one when a golf-ball sized piece of sloppy manure was blasted directly into Billy's open mouth!

His reaction was remarkable. He blinked, gagged and turned green all at the same time. He was trying to talk but we couldn't understand him. It sounded like "Ug mut cow shi mah muth." He was gagging, spitting, sputtering and choking; then he started yakking. He tossed up everything he'd eaten from that day, the day before and I think I saw a candy bar that he'd eaten a month earlier come up. Eventually he stopped heaving and started for Richard with a murderous glare but changed his mind and headed for the river on a dead run. I remembered my toothbrush, got it, and ran after him. I found him on a gravel bar in the river with his head half buried under water. When I was able to talk to him, I offered him my toothpaste and brush, while at the same time was able to convince him it wasn't really Richard's fault. He calmed down but Richard spent the night with one eye open.

DINNER WITH THE BOSS

An incident somewhat similar to the cow pie incident happened to me years later when I attended a dinner party thrown by my boss.

There were assorted appetizers, many of which I'd never seen before. I've always been adventurous when it comes to food, so I picked up an interesting-looking specimen and tossed it into my mouth. I nearly choked! It was horrible . . . some sort of anchovy spread that tasted like it had been out in the sun for a couple of days. I couldn't believe it. I hate anchovies! My wife looked at me and asked, "What's wrong?"

"Ug ink I et somsit," I gagged.

"Well, find the restroom and spit it out," she answered.

Finding the restroom was no easy matter. I was getting sick and was afraid my lunch was going to join the other debris in my mouth. I started to panic but then I spied a half-consumed cup of coffee on the appetizer table. Apparently somebody drank half the cup and was finished with it. I picked up the cup and surreptitiously deposited the offending food from my mouth. I put the cup down and continued to look for the restroom to further cleanse the taste from my mouth.

When I returned I was shocked to find several people huddled around my boss who apparently had suffered some sort of spell. I asked my wife what happened. She said, "I'm not certain. I guess he took a drink from his coffee cup and got sick."

"No kidding? Gee, I wonder what happened? I think I'm going to go out on the patio and see what's going on there."

DINNER AT THE RANCH

I've hunted with a college friend for over twenty years on a beautiful piece of wild land located at the foothills of the Medicine Bow Mountains. This property, which had been a working ranch for many years, still has the old ranch house. It is now used as a hunting ranch by my friend and his friends.

I'm really not a fussy eater but some of the meals we've had at the ranch would challenge a goat.

Dinner usually consisted of a beef or pork roast cooked with vegetables in a large cast-iron kettle on top of an old wood-fired range. Sounds good, right? Not always.

The problem was time. We hunted from daylight to dark, except for a short nap break at noon. To save time we never thoroughly washed the vegetables or cleaned the pot. Each day we would simply toss in another roast to what was left from the last meal, add some casually washed carrots and potatoes and let it go at that. Considering that the previous vegetables also were casually washed and that a number of unwashed fingers had likely found their way into the pot during the last several meals, we had an interesting brew cooking. In addition, occasionally, while preparing the meal, somebody would drop a vegetable or even the roast on the floor, pick it up, haphazardly brush any noticeable dirt or mouse droppings from it and put it back in the pot. I've seen it happen! It would be one thing if the floor was clean but it wasn't. It may have been swept a time or two in the last twenty years but I doubt if it's ever been washed. It wouldn't matter anyway because a whole wild kingdom of rodents lived under the building during the day and practically took the place over at night. Add to that, dog hair, fly parts, cow manure dust from boots and God knows what else, and you get a little idea of what was stewing in that pot about the fifth or sixth day of the hunt.

I never let it bother me. I'd simply put sanitation on hold when I was hunting. Everything in that pot was boiled for a couple of hours each day so I knew it wouldn't kill me. That didn't make it particularly palatable but it was safe. Of course I could have cleaned the kettle myself . . . but then I would have missed my nap.

JIM'S BREAD INCIDENT

One time, at a different Wyoming camp, my friend Jim showed up a day early for the hunt. The food was to arrive the next day so he made a couple of sandwiches at home to bring with him. Unfortunately, about halfway to the camp, he remembered he'd left the sandwiches at home. No problem, he'd almost certainly find something to eat at the camp.

He arrived late in the evening to a dark, cold cabin with no light except a small candle.

He searched everywhere but couldn't find a single thing to eat except a stale loaf of some dark bread, probably left over from the previous fall, that was on the kitchen table. The bread was as hard as a rock but Jimmy was hungry and when Jimmy is hungry, he'll eat almost anything. There was a large kitchen knife lying alongside the bread that had apparently been used the last time someone ate from that loaf. The bread was like a brick but he was able to slice off a small piece and ate it. He remembers thinking, "This is the worst bread I've ever eaten," but he was desperate so he sliced off another piece and then another. Finally, after several slices, he decided the bread was so bad he couldn't eat any more.

The next morning his friends arrived. As Jim was helping them unload their truck he remarked, "I'm starving. I forgot my sandwiches at home and I couldn't find a thing to eat except that stale bread on the kitchen table."

"What stale bread?" they asked.

"That loaf on the table, it's the worst bread I've ever tasted," he answered.

"You ate some of that?" his friend replied incredulously.

"Yeah," Jim answered suspiciously, "why not?"

"Because it isn't bread," he answered, "that's a piece of a manufactured fireplace log that we used to start the kitchen fire. We'd slice little pieces off. Didn't you see the knife?"

"Yeah. That's what I used to slice it."

A MEAL TO REMEMBER

There were other meals at the ranch that were noteworthy, like the time John fried brook trout so hot and so long that by the time he finished they were nothing but pieces of carbon that would shatter if you dropped them, or the Thanksgiving turkey he forgot about that turned into a rock. But we've had some great meals at the ranch as well and I'd like to tell you about the best one ever.

We were hunting elk in Wyoming and staying at John's ranch. The day before we had killed a nice five-point bull, which was now cooling on the meat pole. Since we didn't have to be back in Wisconsin for a couple more days, John suggested we stay an extra day and fish brook trout and hunt blue grouse.

The day was warm but it was cool down in the green-forested canyon bottom through which the creek flowed. The creek was spring fed, crystal clear and so cold it was difficult to hold your

OUTDOOR FOLLIES

hand in it for long. In a couple of hours we had our limit of nice brook trout. We cleaned them at the creek, carried them back to the truck and put them on ice in a cooler.

It was already noon so we snacked on junk food we had brought with us in the truck as we drove to an area where we'd previously seen several flocks of blue grouse. As we were driving along, John suddenly swerved to the side of the road and skidded to a halt. I didn't know what had happened . . . had he seen an elk or bear? I yelled, "what did you see?"

"Shaggymanes," he answered.

Sure enough, alongside the road was a large patch of Shaggymane mushrooms. We filled a paper bag half full of the delicious mushrooms.

It was one of those days when everything went perfect. In a short time we located several flocks of blue grouse and soon had enough for dinner.

We got back to the ranch, dressed the birds and put them on ice. Meanwhile, I removed the tenderloins from the recently cooled elk.

Several friends dropped by and after a couple of rounds of drinks we prepared dinner. We had appetizers of mushrooms and sliced blue grouse rolled in flour and lightly pan-fried in butter. Appetizers were followed by entrees of fried brook trout and sliced fried elk tenderloin served with red wine. Desert was fresh apple pie, baked at the ranch with apples I brought from Wisconsin. A meal fit for a king!

The next morning we were on our way back to Wisconsin hoping that next year we would once again be able to return to the ranch, one of the most beautiful places on the planet Earth.

A MEMORABLE TURKEY HUNT

● ● ● ● ● ● ● ● ● ● ● ● ● ● ● ● ● ● ●

This is not a humorous story. It is a true story about a fabulous turkey hunt by a very inexperienced turkey hunter.

Peter F. Crowley

This story is about the greatest turkey hunt I'll ever have.

I'm an amateur turkey hunter. My turkey calling is limited to "yelps" with a mouth diaphragm. However, I have a couple of friends, Mike and Russ, who are excellent turkey hunters and are willing to call for me.

I've hunted turkeys for five or six seasons and have managed to bag a couple of gobblers, thanks to their help. This year Mike and Russ were only able to hunt with me for the first two days of my planned three-day hunt. They called for me during the first two days but the birds wouldn't talk. We heard a few gobbles at daybreak, but at full daylight the birds stopped gobbling.

Both Mike and Russ shot gobblers on the second day of our hunt, but not in the traditional way. Russ was walking through the woods searching for a new calling location. As he approached the top of a hill, he very cautiously peeked over and was surprised to see a mature tom feeding about thirty-five yards away. He was able to get into position for a shot and got the bird. It weighed twenty-two pounds and was a beauty.

Mike had an exciting and unusual hunt. He called in two groups of toms at the same time. A short distance from him they merged and began feuding. After witnessing a furious fight, he was able to bag one of the toms.

The third day I was on my own. The weather was perfect. It was warm, quiet and clear when it had been wet, windy and cold. I left my pickup before dawn and walked on an old road toward a ridge. I owl hooted a short distance from the truck. No answer. I owl hooted again a couple hundred yards farther up the road and heard two gobbles, one in front and one behind me. The bird behind me was farther away so I decided to go after the bird nearer to me. Meanwhile, an owl hooted a series of six or seven times and both turkeys answered each time. I eased toward the bird in front of me until I thought I was about two hundred yards away and yelped. He answered. We continued our conversation for fifteen minutes, but then he moved away and out of hearing.

Common sense told me to stay put, as I had been told that a tom will eventually come back to investigate what he thought was a hen yelping once he finishes whatever business he happens to be up to at the moment. But curiosity got the best of me and I started moving in the direction from which I had last heard the tom.

I came to a ridge and concluded that the bird may have dropped over the top, and because of that, I might not have been able to hear him from my previous location. The top of the ridge was about fifty yards away and I didn't want to crest the ridge for fear of spooking the tom so I set up where I was and gave a soft yelp.

He answered from near the top of the ridge. He was close, but out of sight. Meanwhile another turkey gobbled to my left about one hundred yards below the ridge. I thought, "I'm in great shape, I've got two birds coming in." I waited awhile and yelped again. Immediately both turkeys gobbled, the one below the ridge sounded closer.

I turned slightly to my left to intercept the bird without completely taking my eye off the ridge. All of a sudden the tom from the ridge appeared, walking toward me below the top of the ridge sixty yards away. When he walked behind a tree, I turned back to my right so I would be in position to shoot when he came abreast of me. He came out from behind the tree, but started angling toward the top of the ridge at a distance of fifty to sixty yards. He walked into a little depression near the top of the ridge and that was the last I saw of him. I had no clue where he went but had to assume he walked over the ridge and down the other side.

OUTDOOR FOLLIES

Meanwhile, I hadn't heard anything from turkey number two, so I decided to yelp. No answer. My guess is that he saw me when I turned to intercept turkey number one and I spooked him. I waited about twenty minutes and decided to crest the hill and see if I could get turkey number one interested again.

I went a short distance over the top and yelped again. The turkey answered from somewhere below the ridge, however, I also heard what I was certain was another hunter yelping from a direction beyond the bird farther below the ridge. Although I was closer to the turkey than the other hunter, I decided to stop calling and place myself directly opposite the turkey from the other hunter and see what developed. The other hunter continued to yelp and the turkey continued to gobble.

Things were quiet for a while, then I heard the bird gobble much farther away and to my left. If I were going to intercept the bird, I would have to move left along the ridge top. Curiously, the other hunter also had quit yelping. I had just gotten situated in my new location when I heard the hunter yelp directly below me. He also had circled in the direction the bird was headed. That caused the tom to reverse direction as I heard him gobble from almost the exact location I had just left. Shortly after that gobble I heard a shotgun blast from the same direction and realized there were two other hunters and they had bagged the bird. What a disappointment! I had come so close.

I was disgusted and decided to vacate the area and go after the second bird I'd heard at daybreak. Not wanting to meet the other hunters, I slipped over and down the ridge far enough away to be out of sight and walked along the ridge side for about two hundred yards. Once I felt comfortable that I was clear of them, I climbed back to the ridge top and yelped.

How surprised I was to hear a gobble right on top of me. I dropped down and got set up. The bird sounded like he was about fifty yards away, slightly to my left and a little down the ridge. The brush was so thick I could only see about thirty yards. I was a little over the top, so I couldn't see at all over the side I had just walked up. The turkey gobbled again, closer. It seemed like he was right on the ridge top, but I couldn't see him. Then another bird gobbled farther down the ridge and to the left. So . . . there were two gobblers. I waited, expecting to see a bird any second, but nothing happened. After a few minutes of silence, I gave a yelp. Both birds answered. The one to my left had moved farther away. The one on the ridge top was very close, but had dropped over the other side of the ridge in a direction that I could only see about ten yards. He sounded directly across from me, working his way along the other side of the ridge and soon would be behind me.

I waited about twenty minutes, occasionally yelping. He would answer off and on but with waning enthusiasm. Meanwhile, the one at the bottom had stopped gobbling altogether. I concluded that there was no possible way the bird near me would come close enough for a shot and that he was losing interest and soon would walk away. I decided to try to poke my head over the top of the ridge. As carefully as I could, I silently sneaked to a position behind a tree where I could raise my head and take a peek. I could see down the hill and to the left, nothing. I carefully glanced to the right and froze. There, not thirty-five yards away, were three mature toms. They were feeding and didn't have a clue I was watching them. However, there was a problem. I am right handed and couldn't shoot in their direction from my position. I never moved until all the birds were looking away from me, then I moved my head back behind the tree and slid my body below the top of the ridge. Ever so slowly, I turned into a shooting position and slowly peeked over the ridge. Sure enough, there they were, pecking away. I got the gun up without being seen and took a bead on the nearest bird.

At this point, my inexperience as a turkey hunter once again manifested itself. I'm told I should have made some sort of turkey noise and the birds would have lifted their heads and looked in my direction so I would have a head shot. Instead, I assumed they were close enough to kill with a body shot. I shot at the nearest bird and was shocked to see all three of them fly away apparently unharmed. I knew I might have been making a mistake even as I shot and now, as I watched them fly away, I was sick. How stupid I was! What an incredible screw-up! I not only didn't get the bird but also may have mortally wounded it.

I was able to watch the birds fly for about one hundred yards and carefully marked the spot where I'd last seen them. I ran to that spot hoping that if the bird were mortally wounded, it might be flopping abound on the ground and if I got there fast enough I would hear it. No luck! After searching for an hour and remembering that on turkeys we had killed in previous years, the shot that had hit the body had barely penetrated the feathers and skin. I felt somewhat comfortable that the bird would survive. I decided to go back on the ridge top and try to get an answer from the bird which had been below me.

I crested the ridge, dropped down about sixty yards toward where I last heard the turkey and gave a yelp. Bingo! He answered right away and seemed to be below me within a couple hundred yards. Also, I thought I heard another tom answer from all the way across the valley on the ridge top beyond. I decided to go after the bird below me and if it didn't work out, I'd go after the bird on the far ridge.

I talked with the bird below me for a while but he didn't seem very interested. Eventually, he wouldn't answer at all and I assumed I'd either been spotted or had called too much. Sneaking into the valley, I called again. There was no answer from either the near bird or the one I thought I'd heard on the far ridge top. It was almost 11:00 a.m. and I figured my turkey hunting was nearly finished for this year. Regardless, I climbed the distant ridge and gave a yelp. Immediately a turkey answered, very close. However, once again it was so brushy I couldn't see very far. I continued to call, but he moved away and eventually quit answering.

It was time to head back. As I headed for my truck, I remembered that I had never really made an effort to go after the second bird I'd heard on the ridge behind me at daylight. No telling where that bird was now but since the ridge was only a short distance out of my way, I headed toward it.

I climbed the ridge on an old tote road which went directly up and over. As I walked the tote road, I yelped just before cresting the top. I was rewarded with a thunderous gobble from a bird which sounded like he was just over the ridge, perhaps thirty yards away. I dropped to my knee, got my facemask on and expected to see the bird at any second.

This situation was the same story as the last two birds; I was twenty yards on one side of the ridge and the turkey was just barely out of my sight on the other. I yelped and the tom answered again. I felt there was a good chance that the bird would come to me so I stepped off the road and knelt down just to the side of and behind a large tree.

I was in a perfect position if the bird moved toward me. I waited a couple of minutes and yelped. Again he answered instantly but sounded like he'd moved more to my right. Regardless, he was still on his side of the ridge but no farther away. I yelped and he answered. Now I was able to pinpoint his direction. He was on the side of the road opposite me and just over the ridge. I wasn't certain what to do. Would he come in? Should I stand up and try to see him? Should I shut up and hope he'd get curious and come for a look? I was uncomfortable that I could only see such a short distance.

Just for the heck of it, I tried a real soft "come here" yelp. The gobbler came unglued! His answer was immediate, loud and angry. It sounded for all the world like he said, "You better get over here . . . right now!" I waited . . . nothing.

The tree I was kneeling behind was large enough so that I could stand up behind it without being seen. If I could do it without making any noise, I could gain some elevation and see farther over the ridge. After waiting a while, I decided I'd take the chance.

I slowly stood up, looked in the direction of the bird and saw some movement. I wasn't certain what I was looking at but knew it had to be the turkey. What I saw looked brown, like the top half of a football. I would see it, then it would become smaller and disappear, then it would get larger, and then smaller again. Finally it dawned on me that the tom was in full strut, walking up and down the hill and all I could see was the top of his fan.

I watched for several minutes but couldn't see his head. I considered making some sort of hen noise, but I wasn't certain I would be able to see his head if he came out of strut. After my last experience, I wanted a full head and neck shot. I watched him walk up and down the hill three times. Then I decided on a new plan. I'd cross the road, sneak five feet along it toward the ridge top to another tree that also appeared to be large enough to hide my entire body. Since I was already positioned next to the road, I figured I could cross the road and make the sneak without being seen.

I waited until he walked down the hill, still in full strut, then ducked down behind the tree, got across the road and hid behind a new tree. He'd been answering every time I yelped so I decided to give a yelp before attempting to get a look at him from my new position. I yelped. He answered. Everything was going according to plan. I didn't attempt to look immediately as I thought he might be watching. After a couple of minutes, ever so slowly and with extreme care, I lifted my head and shoulders while still behind the tree. I was nearly at full height, had my gun ready but still out of sight, when I took a tiny peek. There he was, in full strut, but I still couldn't see his head as he was facing away from me.

I got the gun up and was thinking about making some sort of turkey noise when, suddenly, I was looking directly into the eyes of a turkey with a white, blue and red head and a very suspicious look on his face. I remember thinking, "Well, if you wanted a head and neck shot, you certainly have it now. Take a careful aim." I believe the turkey had me spotted and was just a millisecond from running, but it was too late. I shot and two gobblers flew away. I COULDN'T BELIEVE MY EYES, I MUST HAVE MISSED!!! Then I saw a third bird flopping around in a small depression. My greatest turkey hunt was over.

He was a beautiful bird. His beard was eleven inches long, he weighed twenty pounds and had one inch spurs. Because of the length of his spurs and his weight, I'd guess he was at least three years old. I was as excited as I was when I shot my first buck.

When I got back to my truck and finished admiring, videotaping and photographing him it was almost noon. What an unbelievable morning.

SURVIVAL WHEN ICE FISHING MANUAL

••••••••••••••••••••••••••

The ice fishing on Lake Superior's Chequamegon Bay is good but sometimes treacherous. Ice fishing on Lake Superior is different than ice fishing on a small inland lake. Lake Superior freezes near shore first, then ice forms farther out. Lake Superior rarely freezes over entirely, therefore, under certain conditions, the wind can break off a section of ice and blow it out into open water. Also, because of its large size, it's possible to get lost on it in a snowstorm or fog.

Obviously, ice fishing on Lake Superior can be dangerous. I've had many close calls. Regardless, the fact that I've fished through the ice for over forty years and am still alive is proof that I've got good "ice sense."

Some of my friends disagree, possibly because they've gotten wet while ice fishing with me. They think I'm lucky to be alive. Don't listen to them. Most of them have refused to go ice fishing with me after their first trip and therefore have not had enough opportunities to judge my ice sense. One unhappy experience is not enough.

Given my years of experience, I've decided to write and sell this manual, sharing some of the most important rules of survival while ice fishing. I'm going to call it, "Survival When Ice fishing Manual," or SWIM.

Rule 1. Never Lead!

Whenever you're traveling on the ice, somebody has to lead the way, but why does it have to be you? Why not your fishing partner?

Never volunteer to lead. Often, it may not be an issue. Your fishing partner might be new to the sport and will take the lead simply because you ask him. It's your moral obligation to allow him to do it. Would it be right for you to deprive him of the opportunity to do a good deed? Absolutely not!

You may be fishing with an experienced fisherman, perhaps somebody who has been out with you before. This can be a problem. He may balk at taking the lead. Here are a couple of solutions.

Tell him that you were out in the same area several days ago and caught a lot of fish. Then step back and let greed take over. He will want to rush out ahead of you to find the exact spot where you were fishing in hopes of getting the best fishing location.

If that ruse doesn't work, try this. Say to him, "I forgot to replace the plugs on my snowmobile and it's acting up. I'll have to stop and change them. It won't take me long, just a couple of hours."

Most guys won't want to stand around in the cold while you're changing your plugs, however, if he still hesitates, here's the clincher. Tell him, "I doubt if you can find the spot we're looking for anyway, it's at least a mile north of here." Such a comment will challenge his ability to find a particular location and invoke what I call, "The Daniel Boone Response."

It is a well-known fact that all men believe they are born with a GPS built into their brain and can find any location without help or advice. Invoking The Daniel Boone Response will cause his pride to get in the way of common sense and he'll say, "Of course I can find it. Do you think I just fell off the turnip truck?" and he will then head out in the direction you've indicated.

Rule 2. Beware Of "Nervous Ice."

When you're snowmobiling carefreely along and notice water on the ice, beware! I call this nervous ice. It's nature's way of telling you that there are holes in the ice. Such ice is almost always thin. It's best to proceed carefully when encountering nervous ice . . . usually back in the direction from which you came. It's called a retreat. If you find yourself in this circumstance, feel free to break Rule Number 1 and offer to lead the group, as long as you return the same way you came. In fact, I'd highly advise leading and I wouldn't spend a lot of time discussing the issue. As in most retreats, haste is

OUTDOOR FOLLIES

important. I recommend top speed.

Rule 3. Avoid The "Herd Mentality."

Every year, when the ice first forms, ice fishermen gather together and discuss among themselves whether or not the ice is safe for travel. Nobody wants to be the first one out there! But if one person ventures out, the rest will follow like sheep. I find it amazing that people with otherwise good sense, will venture out on an inch of ice just because somebody else has. Never mind that this first person might be an escapee from a mental institution where he was being treated for suicidal tendencies. If he's on the ice, it's a signal to the herd that all is well and it's safe to follow. I call this the Herd Mentality.

I was once involved in a real-life example of the Herd Mentality. My friend, John, and I were planning to fish an area on Lake Superior called, Little Girl's Point. This area is famous for great lake trout fishing. It's also famous for shifting ice because there are no islands to hold the ice in tight to the shore. A strong offshore wind often will blow the ice out into the open water. Because of this danger, nobody fishes there unless they pull a small aluminum boat along for safety.

One day while John and I were driving to Little Girl's Point to go lake trout fishing, we noticed that a stiff offshore wind had picked up. "That wind is pretty strong," I said, "I think it's going to be too risky to go on the ice." John agreed. Regardless, we drove to the landing just to see if anybody else went out.

Just as we got to the landing, a fisherman named Crazy George was hitching his snowmobile to a fourteen-foot boat preparing to head out on the ice. My friend, John, a mechanical engineer and vice president of a large local company, is a smart guy; however, he took one look at Crazy George and said, "Well, I guess if it's safe enough for him, it's safe enough for us. Let's go."

We were among a dozen parties that rowed back to shore that day. We had succumbed to the Herd Mentality.

Beware of the Herd Mentality! Unless of course, you see somebody catch a fish.

Rule 4. When There's Snow In The Forecast, Bring A Kid.

This is an important rule. Why? Because Lake Superior is a large body of water. It's easy to get lost in snow or fog.

"Oh," you say, "I'm not worried, I have an excellent sense of direction." Yeah sure!

Or, "I have a compass, I can find my way back."

To that I say, "Having a compass is better than nothing, but without a map it's nearly useless. If you get caught in a snowstorm or thick fog, you are completely blinded. It's often difficult to see more than thirty yards in front of you. You have no idea in which direction you're traveling and can quickly become disoriented. I've watched people turn a complete circle before traveling two hundred yards. It can be terrifying. Additionally, the area we fish has many large islands, none of which can be crossed with a snowmobile. Therefore, even if you know the compass bearing back to the landing, you may run into an island along the route. If so, you can never be certain what island it is or at what point you have intersected it. Therefore, you can't be certain which way to go to get around the island and get back on course. There are times when going the wrong way can lead you to open water. Besides, who can remember to bring a compass anyway, not to mention a map?

Just last Saturday, I was talking with my daughter and told her I had forgotten my compass the last time I went ice fishing. I went on to say that I was starting to worry about my memory because the day after I forgot my compass, I left my truck running for four hours. I'd started it so it would warm up, went back in the house to get my hat, got interested in a football game on television and forgot about my truck. Later that same day, I put a roast in the oven and forgot to turn the oven on. Then, that evening, I forgot to sign off the Internet, thereby tying up my phone line for sixteen hours. "Don't worry Dad," she said, "this is nothing new, you've always been forgetful and tend to ramble." Funny, I don't remember being forgetful and I certainly never ramble.

Now, where was I? Oh yes, the only truly safe solution when caught on the ice in snow or fog is a GPS. With a GPS you can safely follow the same route back over which you traveled to get there in the first place. Why bring a seven- year-old kid? First, the batteries in a GPS are always dead when you need to use it. Therefore, you'll need to borrow four of the thirty-five batteries the kid brought with him to energize the various pieces of electronic equipment he deemed necessary for the trip, such as his Game Boy, compact disc player and radio. Second, he's the only person in the group who'll be able to figure out how to use the GPS.

Rule 5. Tricking The Competition.
There will be times when you arrive at your destination and find that others have arrived before you. This is very disturbing. You'd think that fishermen would understand that since you fished there first, you own the spot. Sure, it might have been eight years ago but the statute of limitations on a fishing claim never run out. But no, the minute your back is turned, others sneak in.

This can be a tough problem, especially if they're catching fish. Fortunately, there are a couple of things you can try.

Walk up to them and gaze out away from shore. Then casually mention that you can see open water out there. You won't be lying because Lake Superior rarely freezes across, so there is always open water somewhere. Then tell a gruesome story about fishermen who were fishing at this exact location several years ago when the ice broke off for no apparent reason and they all died of exposure after floating for hours on a piece of broken ice. Mention that you always fish one-half mile closer toward shore in an area where the ice has never broken off and that's where you'll be heading, but first, you felt obligated to warn them of the possible danger they were in. This technique works particularly well if there are inexperienced fishermen in the group.

Don't expect the fishermen to move right away. Paranoia takes time. After a while fear will start eating at them. Meanwhile, set up your shelter one-half mile away. If they're going to move, it'll take about an hour. As soon as they move back toward you, pull up your lines and take their spot. Caution . . . every once in a while you might start catching fish in the area to which you are trying to decoy them. If so, expect company.

Peter F. Crowley

If you are not catching any fish, you must convince them that you are. Yell to one other. Act like you're pulling up fish and run from shelter to shelter. Many fishermen carry walkie-talkies these days. Pull yours out and chatter back and forth with your partner, talking as though you can't keep the fish off your line. If they still don't move, it means they're really into the fish. Then you have no choice but to join them. Start with a casual visit. Explain that the weather conditions have changed and it's unlikely the ice will move. Act as though they're your long lost friends and that it's a joy to see them again. Then start fishing as close to them as your dignity will allow.

Rule 6. Get Your Line Down First.

When lake trout fishing, whoever gets their line down first seems to catch the most fish. I don't know why but it works that way. Therefore, you must get your line down quickly. Other fishermen know this and will try to beat you. Here are a couple of tips to thwart such unsportsman-like activity.

First, always be willing to pick up the bait for the group. That way you can stall giving them their share while you bait up first.

Second, be aware that it's often necessary to chop a hole to check the depth when ice fishing on Lake Superior. Always offer to chop the hole, then, when everybody is satisfied with the depth say, "Well, I might as well stay right here and use this hole." Who can argue with you? After all, you chopped the hole. While others are chopping their holes, you'll be dropping your line down.

Rule 7. Decoying Fishermen.

I'm convinced that there is some sort of unknown signal given whenever a fisherman catches a fish. I know this because every time I catch a fish, another fisherman shows up and starts chopping a hole right next to me. Sometimes, they'll come as close as three or four hundred yards.

I remember one instance in particular. We were among the Apostle Islands near Bayfield, Wisconsin. The exact location was on the south side of Madeline Island, which stretches for thirteen

OUTDOOR FOLLIES

miles and is rarely fished. We could see for miles in all directions and there was nobody in sight. We set up our shelters and started fishing. Shortly thereafter, my fishing partner caught a nice lake trout. He hadn't even gotten his line back down the hole before we heard the whine of a snowmobile. Sure enough, two guys pulled up a short distance away and began setting up their shelters. I mentioned to Bill, "It's incredible, we catch one fish in the middle of nowhere and within ten minutes, somebody's fishing along side of us."

Bill replied, "I swear. I could set up my shelter in the middle of the Sahara Desert and within ten minutes, somebody would be chopping a hole next to me!"

Here's a little trick that will help solve this potential problem. Carry a spruce bough in your equipment and a small container of blood. You can get the blood by wringing out the steak you had for dinner last night. You don't need much, a little goes a long way, something I learned one year when trying to clean up the blood from a minor indiscretion during a bucks-only deer season.

About one quarter mile away from where you intend to fish, chop a hole and fill it with ice so it looks as though somebody had fished there the day before. Then build a little mound of snow and stick the spruce bough in the snow as though it was intended to mark the location. Then, splash a little blood around. Spread it all over and grind it in with your boots until it looks like somebody slaughtered a pig. Then move to where you intend to fish.

If you don't catch any fish ... no problem. Nobody will show up and that will be that. But if you should happen to catch some fish, it's a cinch somebody will show up just as sure as you can expect a raven on a road kill. When zeroing in on you, they will spot the spruce bough. They will not be able to resist running up to it for a look. When they see all the tracks and blood, they'll assume that it's the spot you were looking for but didn't find and they'll set up there.

Rule 8. Retrieval.

What if the worst happens and somebody falls in? Don't panic. You should always carry a length of rope attached to a stick. A two-foot piece of ax handle works nicely. You should practice throwing this device at home, especially if you're planning to fish with me.

Crawl on your belly toward the person in the water until you are close enough so you can accurately throw the stick to him. If this person is somebody who in the past has held back some information from you and if you'd like to have that information, now is an excellent time to ask him. You might also ask him if and where he's been hiding any money, only because you are concerned that the money should go to his next of kin in the event the worst should happen. You might be thinking that such comments are a form of extortion. Nothing could be farther from the truth. These comments are necessary and work in two ways. First they enrage the person and drive his body temperature up several degrees, thereby holding off hypothermia, sometimes for hours. In fact, I've actually seen some people steam. Second, you might learn something useful. Caution! Do not attempt this technique on large, healthy, hotheaded individuals, especially if they have a history of retribution.

Once you throw the stick to him and he grabs it, pull him back onto the ice. Advise him not to stand up. Keep pulling him across the thin ice until he reaches ice strong enough to stand on.

That about sums it up. I've spent a lifetime learning these little tricks and I hope they help you. I'd especially like to cash in on them right now because I need a new snowmobile and I'm a little short of cash, we retired folks being on a fixed income and all. Oh, did I mention to you that I forgot to follow Rule Number 1 last winter? You'd think I'd know better after all these years but I got carried away. A guy at the landing told me about a location where he really caught a lot of fish the day before and I tried to beat him to it.

BIG HILL

· · · · · · · · · ·

Just recently, I enjoyed an afternoon watching my two grandsons sledding. Both of the boys wore protective helmets, expensive snowmobile suits and warm, high-tech mittens. They were sledding on a hill monitored by the city and their mother was standing nearby watching carefully.

I couldn't help but compare that scene to a typical sledding scene from my youth.

There were no city sledding hills, unless you count sledding down a hill on a busy city street. The only reason there was a hill there in the first place was because the road had been elevated so automobiles could cross a set of railroad tracks that had been there before the road was built.

We had plenty of exciting moments on that hill dodging automobiles, not to mention an occasional train. It was exciting for the motorists too. I will always remember the terrified look on their faces when they spotted us at the last second and barely managed to swerve to avoid hitting us. And the language! You'd think they just got off a troop ship. No wonder I have trouble getting through a sentence nowadays without relying on one or two slang words.

"You stupid 'bleeping' kids!" they'd yell. "Do your parents know what you're doing?"

"Yeah, sure," I'd mutter under my breath, "my parents always suggest that I should go out and play in the street." No, of course they didn't know what I was doing . . . at least, I don't think they did. That's just the way it was in those days. People were more inclined then to turn their kids loose and let them take care of themselves than they are today.

Our clothing was pretty "low-tech." I had one winter coat. It had belonged to two other kids before it got to me. I wore the same coat to school, church and sledding, and when I went ice fishing with my dad. Nobody wore long underwear, except my dad, who worked outside all day supervising the loading of boxcars at the local paper mill. He wore long underwear every day of the year. His only concession to the summer heat was to cut the sleeves off six inches below the shoulder.

When we kids needed more warmth, we simply wore two pair of pants. My boots were nothing to brag about either, just shoes and overshoes. If the weather got extremely cold, we'd cut cardboard and put it in the bottom of the overshoes. My feet were always cold when I was a kid, especially when I was ice fishing with my dad. "My feet are freezing," I'd complain.

"Aw, quit yer squawking," he'd answer. "If your feet are cold, take a walk, that'll warm you up."

"I don't wanna take a walk, unless it's to go home," I'd say. "Why don't we get off this block of ice?"

"If you didn't want to come with me, why didn't you say so before we left? Now that we're out here, we're going to stay a while. The fish have just started to bite," was his typical answer.

The best articles of clothing we owned were our hats and mittens, which were knitted by my mother from heavy wool yarn.

I did a lot of sledding in the winter when I was growing up. The best location was a hill that we called "Big Hill." It started at the top of a large ravine and ended at Bay City Creek, which ran through the bottom of the ravine.

Big Hill was located above a point where the Creek had just finished a sweeping curve and then started a long straightaway. It was possible to sled from the top of the Hill to the top of the Creek bank, a distance of about three hundred yards, then, if you were careful, you could take a gentle right turn and continue along the Creek bank for another hundred yards, stopping in the valley below. If you weren't careful and couldn't make the turn, you had to jump off the sled or risk going over the Creek bank.

The Creek was usually dry during the winter. Regardless, it had high banks, which had been created by spring floods during years

OUTDOOR FOLLIES

gone by. If you happened to go over the top of the bank, you had a sheer drop of ten to fifteen feet to the rocks in the Creek bed below. The top of the banks themselves were about fifty feet across.

If that wasn't enough, a railroad track ran above Big Hill. The railroad bed was about thirty feet above the top of the Hill and was higher than Big Hill because it had to access a railroad tressel that crossed Bay City Creek several hundred yards farther down the track.

Most of us were happy to start our sledding from the top of Big Hill, but once in a while an adventurous person would climb the steep embankment up to the railroad tracks for a steeper start. It was like coming down an Olympic ski jump. The embankment was called "Suicide Hill" because there was a good chance you'd take a spectacular fall if you dared to go down it.

Surprisingly, very few people got hurt. There were a few kids that went home with bruises, limps and an occasional lame arm, which was amazing given the wide array of contrivances that barreled down that Hill. There were skis, toboggans, sleds and car hoods. The car hoods were the most dangerous. Sliding down a hill on an inverted car hood was like riding on a meat cleaver. That nobody ever got seriously injured by those car hoods is a testament to the quickness and resiliency of youth. Somehow the riders were always able to bail out at the last second. I wiped out many times on that Hill but walked away every time.

One of the dumbest stunts I ever saw on Big Hill was when a kid rode down with his head stuck under the curl of a toboggan.

His name was Norman. Norman wasn't the brightest bulb in the box but he was what I would call a "gamer." He always wanted to chum around with the older kids; felt it gave him status. I learned later that this same type of behavior is often exhibited in the business world; it's called "suckin' up."

One day, the older boys were taking a six-person toboggan down the Hill. Norman saw them and asked if he could go along. One of the less-gifted of the older boys, George, told Norman that if he wanted to ride with them, he would first have to prove himself.

"How?" Norman asked.

"You have to make the 'Kamikaze run,'" he answered.

"What's the Kamikaze run?" Norman asked.

"It's simple," George said. "All you have to do is lay down and put your head inside the curl of the toboggan and slide down the Hill."

"But I won't be able to see," Norman replied.

"I know, that's why we call it the Kamikaze run. We've all done it," he said, winking to his friends.

Norman was hesitant, but decided to do it anyway.

He laid down, tucked his head under the curl of the toboggan and started down the Hill. As soon as he hit the steep part of the Hill he took off like he was shot out of a cannon. Sure enough, he started heading directly toward the edge of the Creek bank.

"Jump! Jump!" we all yelled, but he didn't jump. He hit the bank and flew through the air, headed for the Creek bed.

"Holy cow, George, I think you killed him!" someone yelled.

"Jeez, it ain't my fault, I thought he would jump," George moaned.

We ran toward the bank over which he had disappeared, expecting to find a broken body. Peeking cautiously over the bank, we were relieved to see Norman, shaken but sitting up. Incredibly, the toboggan had landed between two large boulders in a couple of feet of soft snow. Other than being a little dazed, Norman never had a scratch.

"Wow!" he said, "now I know why you call it the Kamikaze run." He spent the rest of that day enjoying himself riding down the Hill with the older boys.

One day, a friend, Richard, and I walked to Big Hill for an afternoon of sledding. When we got there, we met another friend, Tommy, who was busy building some sort of contraption.

Tommy was the adventurous type, which is why he spent much of his early life with a cast on an arm or leg.

"What are you doing, Tommy?" I asked.

"Building a sling," he answered.

"A sling? What for?" I replied.

"I'm gonna try to jump the Creek with my dad's skis. Look

down there, just before the straightaway, the bank on this side is higher than the bank on the other side. If I can get up enough speed, I think I can jump across the Creek."

"Tommy," I said, "you're nuts! You'll kill yourself."

"Naw, that far bank is filled with snow. If I happen to hit it, I'll have a soft landing."

"Soft landing, like hell! What's the sling for?"

"I don't think I can get enough speed from Suicide Hill and Big Hill; I'll need a boost. That's what the sling is for," he replied.

He had a half dozen old automobile inner tubes that he had cut and tied together end to end. He planned to tie the ends of this inner tube "chain" to the bottom of a couple of old fence poles that were situated about ten feet down from the top of Suicide Hill, then stretch the center of the connected inner tubes to the railroad tracks and tie them to a railroad spike with a rope. Just below the railroad bed was a flat area that everybody used as a jumping-off spot to start their run down the Hill. Tommy's plan was to stand in front of the stretched inner tubes and when he was ready, ask somebody to cut the rope for him. Since he was standing just below the rail bed, the stretched tubes would catch him across his butt and sling him down the Hill. It was just like a big slingshot. He hoped the added momentum from the sling would propel him down the Hill fast enough to jump the Creek.

"I'll tell you what, Tommy. You try that nuthouse device and I guarantee that we'll be visiting you in the hospital," I said.

"We'll see," he replied. "You'll be begging me to use my sling. In fact, if you treat me real nice, I might let you have the first chance to try it."

"Oh, gee! Would you really? You're so kind. But the truth is, I wouldn't get in front of that thing for a million bucks!"

Tommy enlisted our help and the three of us pulled the sling back toward the tracks. It was all we could do to stretch it that far. The sling was as tight as a bow string. It was a miracle that we managed to get it tied to the spike.

Because of the angle, the sling followed the contour of the Hill and was only an inch above the ground. Tommy had it situated perfectly. It appeared that when standing just below the railroad bed, the sling would catch the skier just below the waist.

"Tommy," I said, " that thing is going to break your back. If it doesn't, there's a pretty good chance you'll end up on the moon."

"Nope. I've got it calculated. The sling has to free fly about three feet before it hits me so it has enough speed to do any good. I think I can handle the shock. Once my weight is in the sling it will slow down and should propel me at just the right speed to make the jump."

"You're crazy," I replied.

Just then, Richard looked down along the railroad tracks toward town and saw somebody walking in our direction. "Hey, who's that?" he said.

"Crap!" Tommy said. "That's Rhino Dumbinski."

Rhino wasn't his real name but that's what everybody called him. He was big, dumb and mean. He talked out of the side of his mouth with a snarl, always had a sneer on his face and habitually picked on kids smaller than him. He was older than us and whenever he was around, there was trouble.

"Quick," Tommy said, kicking snow over the sling, "I don't want him to see it."

"Why?" I asked.

"I dunno," Tommy answered, "Rhino's a pain. He'll have something to say about it. Help me kick snow over it and be careful so he doesn't notice what we're doing."

We were able to kick enough light snow over the inner tubes to camouflage them well enough so Rhino would probably not notice the sling.

Rhino sauntered up to us and sneered, "What are you punks up to?"

"Oh nothing," I replied, "just punk stuff."

"Crowley, you got a smart mouth on you. You better watch what you say," he snarled out of the side of his mouth.

That was true enough. My wise mouth had often gotten me into trouble. I had to be a little careful with Rhino; I wasn't about to start a fight with him. On the other hand, Tommy rarely said much but he

OUTDOOR FOLLIES

was one of those small, wiry kids you could never be sure about. One thing for sure, Rhino might frighten him but Tommy wasn't the kind of kid who would turn and run.

Rhino gave us his best sneer and snarled again, "I said, what you punks doing?"

"Nothing," Richard replied.

"Actually," Tommy said, "I was just about to try my dad's skis. That spot, right there," he pointed directly in front of the sling, "is the only place left on the hill that hasn't been all tracked up and I'm going to use it to try these skis."

"Oh yeah, pip-squeak. I just got these new skis," he said, gesturing to his feet, as he put on his skis, "and I'm gonna be the first one down in that new snow."

"Hey," I said, "you can't jump in front of somebody. Wait your turn."

I moved to my left and Rhino moved toward me, directly in front of the hidden sling, preparing to ski down the Hill. Before he started, he looked at me with a malevolent glare and said, "I warned you about your big mouth. You better keep it shut or I'm gonna stick this ski pole in your foot."

"By all means, sir," I said in a mocking tone. "Please allow us to move aside so you can take the Hill. I'm sure we're all happy that you're willing to try this particular spot before us, however, I feel I must warn you that you're likely to find it treacherous. It may be in your best interest to let Tommy go first."

"You wise little creep!" he said, his voice rising in anger. "I warned you about smarting off to me. Now I'm gonna stick this ski pole in your foot."

Something in his tone told me I had crossed the line and that he was serious about stabbing my foot. I'll never know if he would have or not because just as he raised his pole to make the thrust, Tommy cut the rope holding the sling.

It worked perfectly. Rhino was just far enough from the tracks so the sling rose and hit him squarely in the butt. It was spectacular. One second he was standing there and the next, he was catapulted down the hill. "HOLY Shiiieeeeeee," his scream echoed as he blasted down the hill. He was nearly airborne until he reached the point where Suicide Hill blended into Big Hill. He hit the top of Big Hill with a glancing blow before flying over the edge and skiing out of control down Big Hill towards the Creek.

"Wow!" Tommy yelled. The sling worked perfectly. I told you it would."

"You might want to check with Rhino on that," I replied.

"I don't think Rhino's gonna want to talk with us for a while," he answered.

Meanwhile, Rhino looked like an Olympic downhill ski racer who was out of control. Incredibly, he managed to stay on his feet as he rocketed toward the Creek bank.

Tommy got into the spirit of the occasion yelling, "Bend your knees! Bend your knees!"

"I don't care what he bends, Tommy, he's a goner," I remarked.

As Rhino neared the bank, he realized that because of his speed, he couldn't negotiate a right turn, nor could he risk a fall. The best he could hope for was to jump the bank and survive the landing.

From our high vantage point, we could see it all. It was a thing of beauty. He was a heck of a lot better on skis than I would have guessed. He cleared the near bank with a scream and nearly, very nearly, cleared the other bank.

Alas, he landed about six inches short. Well, that is, his skis landed six inches short. From then on, the laws of physics took over. His feet were torn from the bindings and his body flew over the top of the bank into the snow and brush.

"Wow!" Tommy said. "I think he would have made it if he would have jumped just as he left the bank. Did you see the snow fly and the brush break when he cartwheeled into the woods. That was something!"

"I wonder if he got hurt?" Richard asked.

"Naw," Tommy said, "he's too dumb to get hurt. We better take a look but I don't want to get too close."

"That's the smartest thing I've ever heard you say," I replied.

As we started down the Hill, we heard a roar from the other side of the Creek. "I'm gonna kill you guys!"

"Well," Tommy said, "the good news is that he's alive. The bad news is that he doesn't sound very happy."

We watched as he walked out of the brush toward his skis. "Look what you've done to my skis," he blubbered. "My brand new skis!"

I was actually starting to feel sorry for him and said so.

"I'll tell you what, Pete," Tommy said, "he got exactly what he deserved. He's always punching somebody smaller than him. He was going to stab you in the foot with his ski pole. As far as I'm concerned, he got off easy." Then, he cupped his hands to his face and yelled, "Rhino! It's Tommy. I'm the one who built the sling and sprung it on you. If you mess with us again, next time you won't be able to walk home."

"Jeez, Tommy. You're gonna get us killed," I said.

"Naw, he won't do anything. He's just a bully. He won't mess with us. Even so, I think we better steer clear of him for a while."

"Good plan," I said, and we did.

CAMP ORIENTA

•••••••••••••••••••

In Wisconsin, deer season is known as "Holy Week." Schools close, businesses slow down and a million hunters take to the woods on opening day.

I am no exception. I love whitetail hunting. I spend much of my time in the spring and summer scouting for deer and when I'm not doing that, I'm reading books and articles about deer and deer hunting.

Given the amount of time I've put into deer hunting, you'd expect me to be pretty good at it. I think I am. My friends disagree, but what do they know? Regardless, you don't have to be good at deer hunting to enjoy it. It's like golf; poor players often enjoy the game more than good players.

There's plenty of public land where I live and I've always been able to find remote areas in which to hunt. I'd get up long before daylight and walk miles into the wilderness, often not returning until after dark. This system worked well because I was able to get away from most hunters. However, my son didn't share my fanatical enthusiasm for walking deep into the woods. Still, he wanted to hunt.

"Are you serious, Dad? You want to start hunting before daylight and be in the woods all day. Can't we find a place close to the road, hunt in the morning, get our deer and go home? Running around in the brush all day is crazy. Besides, I've made some walks with you. You never walk in a straight line and we usually end up corkscrewing our way from the truck to the stands. You claim we're not lost but I get the feeling that you never know exactly where we are."

He was right about that. One time he had been with me when we had walked in circles while looking for a blueberry patch that I'd picked the day before. Another time, we got screwed up trying to find a remote section of a trout stream and were lost for five hours.

I can usually find my way to where I want to go, but not always in a straight line. When I'm in the woods, I should never take a step without having my compass in my hand, but I do. Consequently, I get turned around from time to time. I'm not troubled by that, in fact, I never consider myself lost. I may not know precisely where I am at any given moment, but when I want to go home, I simply take a compass bearing toward my vehicle and walk out. A few times, I've forgotten that compass bearing back to the truck. Now that can be a problem.

I've always had trouble with direction. Once, when my daughter was six years old, I took her along on a summer deer scouting trip. I planned to drive on some old logging roads near the area where I was planning to hunt that fall to look for deer sign. We were a half mile from the main road when I had to answer a "call-of-nature." I left my daughter in the truck and walked just far enough into the brush to be out of sight. When I was finished, I started walking back to the truck. I couldn't find it! Somehow, I had gotten turned around. I was in a panic because I was afraid my daughter might try to follow me, as I had told her I would only be gone a few minutes. I ran through the woods and eventually came out on the main road. Thank God! I quickly found the logging road on which the truck was parked and ran back to it as fast as I could. Thankfully, my daughter, although frantic, was still waiting for me.

So, my son had a point. Still, I wanted him to hunt with me, but he put up such a fuss about spending full days in the woods and taking long hikes that I needed to find a compromise. After thinking it over, I decided that the best solution would be to hunt from a cabin. Then he could hunt as much as he liked and return to the cabin whenever he wanted and I'd be free to roam.

The problem was that I didn't own a hunting cabin or any land on which to build one. The solution was to find a wealthy friend who owned a large piece of land with a hunting cabin on it and worm myself in. Not an easy thing to do.

As luck would have it, I met such a person at a party during the early fall. Bill was a deer hunting fanatic. Also, his son, David, was about the same age as my son. He wasn't wealthy, at least not any longer because he'd just mortgaged his life to purchase the best piece of wild land in northern Wisconsin. He'd built a hunting cabin on it during the summer and named it "Camp Orienta," because it was located in the town of Orienta. During the party, we talked endlessly about deer hunting and his land purchase. "The land you bought is perfect for deer hunting," I said. "I could never afford such a purchase."

"Sure you could," he replied. "All you have to do is mortgage everything you own, ask your wife to take a second job, cut your grocery bill in half, get rid of the phone and TV, keep your car for twenty-five years and ask your kids if they would mind delaying their college education for forty or fifty years. It's easy."

"Yeah," I said, "but what about the cost of a divorce."

"That could be a problem for some people but not for me. Karen thinks the land purchase was a great idea. Don't you, Karen?"

"Yeah, sure. If we get a chance, let's buy the Queen Mary too," she said, rolling her eyes.

"See?" Bill answered, "What did I tell you?"

Actually, Bill's wife, Karen, really didn't care. Karen's a good artist. Like many creative people, she isn't caught up in material things. Being involved in her artwork and raising happy children were her priorities. Money in the hand, as long as there was enough to get by, was secondary. Bill could worry about the financial end of things. If he wanted to buy wild land, that was fine with her, as long as there was a roof over her head, food on the table and lots of materials for her art projects.

"Bill," I said, "how would you feel about Bob and I joining you and David at Camp Orienta this coming deer season?"

He never hesitated. "That would be great," he said.

That was thirty years ago and my son and I haven't missed a season yet.

We've had many exciting times at Camp Orienta. Our boys shot their first bucks there and have each taken a trophy bear. While growing up, they have allowed Camp Orienta to become part of their lives and culture. Both of the boys are grown now and have their own lives and careers. Regardless, every deer season, for the last thirty years, we've been together at Camp Orienta. Once, shortly after my son started a new position with IBM, Bill asked him if he was going to be able to get off for deer season. Bob answered that he would either be off for deer season or he would quit his job at IBM.

Bob isn't as serious about deer hunting as I am. In fact, one season he didn't even get out of bed until noon on opening day. Regardless, he shows up every year on the day before the season opens. I used to push him to hunt harder, now I'm just happy that he shows up. I don't care if he hunts or not.

Having our sons with us was important, but as they grew up, went away to school and started their own lives, they were only at the camp during the deer season. On the other hand, Bill and I forged a solid friendship and have spent much of our time during the past thirty years scouting for deer, planting food plots, fishing, baiting bear, working on the camp, bow hunting and muzzle loader hunting at Camp Orienta. Now that we're both retired, we spend even more time there.

Camp Orienta is located fifteen miles north of Iron River, Wisconsin. It is eight hundred and eighty three acres of pristine whitetail habitat. This remote piece of land is unique because the only road leading to it ends right at the camp. The land is bordered on the east by the Iron River, a blue ribbon trout stream, and on the south, west and north by private land; therefore, there are no roads bordering the property except the access road. Today, it's impossible to find such a piece of land in northern Wisconsin as remote and wild as Camp Orienta.

The first deer season that Bill and his son and I and my son hunted at Camp Orienta will be forever etched in our memories.

Bill had constructed a main cabin then added a separate sauna building on the property. The buildings were well built. Bill's Finnish heritage and engineering background saw to that. In fact, the roof trusses could probably support fifteen feet of wet snow and the door on the cabin, which he made, had enough lumber in it to build a small house. The problem was that he hadn't had time to finish the cabin by deer season. In fact, even today, thirty years later, it still isn't completely finished. Every deer season we talk about the improvements we're going to complete during the following summer, but somehow they never all get done. Nevertheless, little by little, the cabin is improving. Today, it's nothing like it was in the early years.

That first year there was no insulation or siding, and to say it was drafty was an understatement. In fact, on windy days it was difficult to keep a match burning long enough to light the Franklin fireplace we used to heat the cabin. That Franklin fireplace, which we used for twenty years, was already fifteen years old that first season. Anybody who has ever tried to heat a building with a Franklin fireplace knows they're designed for looks, not heat. We spent a lot of time that first season huddled around that stove. Within forty-eight inches of the stove, it was fairly warm, beyond that, it chilled off pretty fast, especially in cold weather.

The cabin had a one-room lower level with a stairway leading to a loft above. We slept in the loft on mattresses laid on the floor, Bill and David on one side, Bob and I on the other.

It was unusually cold that first season. The temperature dipped to well below zero and we struggled to stay warm at night after the fire went out. The heat rose to the loft and we were comfortable when we turned in, but during the night the temperature in the building slowly dropped. By morning, there was ice in the wash basin. Bill and I would get up well before daylight and I'd get the fire going while Bill started breakfast. The boys stayed in their sleeping bags until we bullied them out after the cabin was warmed up and breakfast was ready. During the day, the boys, especially Bob, would be back at the camp often enough to keep the fire going.

During the late summer, the flies were unbelievable! Millions of them. They're called cluster flies and apparently crawl into any crack or corner of a building to winter-over. When we opened the cabin, which hadn't been opened for several weeks, we found a layer of flies an inch thick. I'm serious! We swept and vacuumed them up but as soon as we got a little heat in the building, more of them would crawl out of the cracks and start buzzing around. They were everywhere; in the toaster, our coffee, food, dishes and sleeping bags. At night, while it was still warm in the loft, it wasn't wise to sleep on your back with your mouth open, unless you wanted flies for dessert that is. Eventually, I got used to them but I never liked it. Years later, we started having the building sprayed, which solved the problem.

Curiously, Bill had not nearly finished constructing the main building when he started building the sauna, which is another indication of a Finnish heritage. A Finn's house might be ready to cave in, but the sauna building is usually in good working condition.

Bill's sauna building was constructed with the same strong materials as the cabin, except the sauna room itself was finished in cedar. The building had a dressing room, storage room, sauna room and a covered deck. The sauna room was about seven by twelve with three benches. The floor was constructed from cedar that was cut in a mosaic pattern. Don't ask me why . . . it must have taken days to cut that perfectly matched pattern, when it would have been just as easy to slap pine boards down and cut a hole in them for the drain. The door was wider than a normal door and was also homemade of heavy materials. If we ever need to build another cabin, we could construct it by tearing apart the doors on the cabin and sauna building. I believe the sauna could take a direct hit from a category five tornado and survive. Like I say, saunas are important to the Finn's.

The evenings were fun and relaxing. We had a table and chairs situated near the fireplace where Bill and I would have a couple of drinks, discuss the day's hunt, prepare a meal and talk about where we would hunt the next day.

Bill was also trapping mink in those days and while we were talking, he would skin, stretch and hang their hides from the rafters. It gave the cabin a different look and feel, as though we were in a remote trapping cabin a hundred years earlier. While we were doing that, the boys would build a fire in the sauna stove and take a sauna. Then we'd all sit down to a big dinner. After dinner, Bill and I would grab a couple of beers and take a sauna while the boys read and lounged around.

The boys often had the sauna temperature well over two hundred Fahrenheit degrees and we were able to soak up enough heat to feel comfortable standing outside nude in below zero temperatures. I'd stay in the sauna until I was half cooked. Then I would walk out and stand on the deck to cool off. It was enjoyable listening to the night sounds and looking at the moon and the stars. Over the years, I've heard a variety of birds and animals from the sauna deck at night, including timber wolves, owls, bobcats and coyotes.

Regardless of how cold we got during the day, we were always warm and cozy after taking a sauna. After tramping around in the woods all day and having a few "snorts," a big meal and a hot sauna, I never had any trouble sleeping nights while at Camp Orienta.

On the opening morning of deer season, we were in the woods before daylight. I felt that Bob was still too young to wander around in the woods on his own, so I insisted that he stay close to me. We worked our way slowly north along an old logging road to a point where the road overlooked a large ravine. It was a good spot to watch for deer and since it was on the logging road leading directly to the cabin, it was hard to get lost. I put Bob there with strict instructions not to move until I came back.

After hunting a couple of hours, I decided I'd better check on Bob. When I got to where I had left him, he was gone! I looked all over but couldn't find him. I yelled but he didn't answer. There was no snow, so I couldn't follow his tracks. Therefore, I had no clue where he had gone. Had he decided to look for me? Had he seen a deer and tried to follow it? I had no idea. I was frantic. Why the heck did I ever leave him alone?

I searched all around, practically running from place to place but couldn't locate him.

I ran into Bill and told him what happened. "He probably got cold and went back to the cabin, I wouldn't worry," he said.

"I don't think so," I answered, "I gave him firm instructions to remain here until I came back."

Finally, after exhausting all other options, I decided to go back to the cabin, although I was certain he wouldn't have returned there without telling me. Bob was usually pretty dependable so I had good reason to be concerned. I ran most of the way, worried sick. When I got there, sure enough, there he was, lying on his mattress reading a magazine. I exploded at him.

"What the heck are you doing here? Didn't I tell you not to leave that spot without telling me?"

"I told you. Didn't you see my note?" he answered.

"What note? I never saw any note!"

"I wrote it with a bullet on a piece of birch bark and stuck it in a knot hole on a tree near where I was standing."

"You did what? How in the world did you expect me to find a note like that?" I exclaimed.

"Gee, I don't know, Dad. You should have looked, it was right there in plain sight."

"I'll tell you what. If you ever pull a dumb stunt like that again, I'll wring your neck. When I tell you to stay put . . . stay put!"

I was so relieved to find him that I couldn't remain angry. Later that day, when I walked by his stand, sure enough, there was the note.

Bill shot the first buck at Camp Orienta. A nice heavy eight pointer. It was a beauty. He and David dragged the deer back to the camp and hung it in a nearby spruce tree.

Late the next day, Bill was standing next to his deer looking thoughtfully.

"Hey, Pete," he said, "I want to have this deer mounted and it's already half frozen. I won't be able to skin it if it's completely frozen. I wonder if we can hang it in the cabin?"

"In the cabin?" I asked.

"Yeah, it won't be in the way, we can walk around it," he answered.

"I don't care," I said, amused by the prospect of having a deer hanging in the cabin. It would make a nice addition to the other critters that were already hanging there.

We did it. We actually hung the deer in the cabin. People don't believe me but I have photos to prove it. All season long we were banging into that deer while walking from the refrigerator to the table and back again. That deer and the mink, mingled with the cooking aroma, combined into an odor I'll always associate with Camp Orienta.

OUTDOOR FOLLIES

David was the next to score. He was sitting in a blind that he and his father had built before the season when he heard a grunting noise. He didn't know what it was; it sounded like a pig coming through the brush. He listened and watched, when suddenly a doe came trotting into view. Then, to his amazement, he saw a nice eight-point buck following her. The noise David had heard was the buck grunting every couple of steps as he trailed the doe. Bang! David had his first buck. Bill arrived a few minutes later and enjoyed a special, never to be repeated, moment with his son.

I shot a small buck the next day but my son still hadn't scored. This was his first year of deer hunting so I wasn't surprised. He might have been though, because I think he thought getting a deer would be easier. He put in a decent effort the first couple of days but now he was beginning to lose interest. It was becoming more and more difficult to get him up each morning.

On the second to the last day of the season, I found an area in the northwest corner of Bill's property that was full of fresh deer sign. A strong wind had blown down several large spruce trees and the deer were feasting on the moss that grew high up on the branches that they were now able to reach. I decided to build a blind and take Bob there the next morning. When I finished the blind, it was late in the day and as I was leaving, I saw several deer working their way toward the downed timber. This was going to be a great stand in the morning. The problem was that it was a long walk from the cabin and I knew Bob would be reluctant to get up early enough to give us extra time to walk to the blind before daylight. I'd have to work on him.

At first, he flat out refused to go. "Jeez, Dad, I'm tired. Let's sleep in and hunt around the cabin for a while."

"Bob, this spot is hot. You have a great chance for a buck. It looks as good as any spot I've seen all season," I answered.

He bellyached about it, but I painted such a rosy picture that he finally agreed to get up early and hike with me to the blind.

I got up at 3:30 a.m. Bill, like the good friend he is, got up with me even though he wouldn't be doing much hunting that day. When I looked at the thermometer, I had second thoughts; it was five degrees below zero, very cold if you're planning to sit in a blind for any length of time. Regardless, it was the last day and the last chance for Bob to get a buck. I decided to wake him up. I woke him up at 4:00 a.m., then again at 4:15 a.m., and 4:30 a.m. When he still didn't get up at 4:30 a.m., I threatened to pour a pail of water on him. I meant it too. That got him moving. He grumbled and groaned but finally got up and started to dress.

After a hasty breakfast, we started walking to the blind. We got there just as daylight was breaking. We were filled with anticipation. After watching for two hours without seeing any deer, my spirits began to sag. I was freezing and I knew Bob had to be cold also, but surprisingly, he never complained. I think that I had painted such a great picture, he was convinced a buck would eventually show up. I was disappointed and disgusted, it would have been better to wait until evening, a better time to see feeding deer but I'd have a hard time talking Bob into coming back if we didn't see anything this morning.

About nine a.m. I had to answer a "call-of-nature." I told Bob that I would be gone about a half hour and would make a big circle around the blind and try to scare a deer toward him. I told him that if he didn't see one by the time I got back, we would quit.

"Ok," he said.

I took off, got done what I needed to get done and started to make a circle. I made what I thought was a circle and should have been back to the blind but I couldn't find Bob. I should have been able to see his fluorescent orange from at least one hundred yards away but he was nowhere in sight. I was certain he would not have left the blind, especially after the tongue lashing I gave him when he left the stand on the first day. Then it dawned on me, incredibly, I had gotten turned around exactly the same way I did when my daughter was waiting for me in the truck!

This time I had an advantage because there was snow. I decided to backtrack along the same trail I'd walked on to get where I was . . . wherever that might be. I'd just started walking when I heard a loud "bang!" followed by another shot. It had to be Bob shooting. The shots were only a couple of hundred yards away and somehow, I knew that Bob had shot his first buck. I can't describe how excited I was as I hurried toward the sound of the shots.

"Bob, where are you?" I yelled.

"Over here, Dad, I got one!"

I couldn't believe what I was hearing as I ran toward the sound of his voice. Finally, I saw him standing over a nice eight-point buck. I was ecstatic. After I gave him a congratulatory hug he told me the story.

After I was gone over half an hour, he suspected I'd gotten turned around but decided to stay put because of all the fuss I'd made the last time he moved without being told to. He figured I'd eventually find him. Suddenly, he saw a deer. As he watched it walk toward him, he saw it was a buck! It didn't appear to be in a hurry, just moving slowly toward him. He waited until it was twenty yards away before he shot. The deer went down immediately but he shot again just to be certain.

We stayed by the deer for a long time, savoring the moment. I asked him to repeat the story because I didn't want to miss a single part. Finally, I dressed the deer for him and we started the long drag back to the cabin. It took us most of the day to drag the deer back to the cabin but I was so excited that I never noticed.

It was the first of many bucks that we would drag to the cabin together but this one was the best. It would always be the highlight of our deer hunting together. Today, thirty years later, Bob and I have a close relationship but we were never closer than we were on the last day of the first season we hunted at Camp Orienta when he shot his first buck. In the years that followed, he started maturing and growing into his own person. He would never again be that young boy, sharing a special moment with his father at Camp Orienta.

I have a photo in my home of Bob with that first deer. I look at it often and dream of days gone past.

Later that day, Bill and David and Bob and I reminisced about the season. It had been a great one, no doubt about that. A season of many firsts. What we didn't know then is that it was only the beginning of an incredible run of outdoor excitement that isn't over yet, thirty years later, at Camp Orienta.

BEARING UP UNDER FATHER

I have never seriously considered myself lazy but I try to make a practice of avoiding unnecessary work when possible. So why was I stumbling through a swamp on Labor Day weekend with sweat running down my face, swatting at hoards of mosquitoes while hauling a sixty-pound load of stale sweet rolls on my back?

I was bear hunting. To be precise, I was bear baiting, a preliminary to bear hunting I can learn to live without.

Thinking back to that July preceding our first bear hunt, I realize that I should have been at least slightly suspicious when Dad casually mentioned, "I think I'll hunt bear at Camp Orienta this fall. Do you want to go with me?"

Camp Orienta is a cabin on eight hundred and eighty three acres of wild land that is owned by my dad's friend, Bill. My dad and I and Bill and his son, David, had been hunting deer there for the past several years. It was great fun being there during deer season and I reasoned that bear hunting would be similar, so I told him, "Yes."

How was I to know that bear hunting meant we would spend weeks sweltering in the sun trying to feed half of the northern Wisconsin bear population?

When it was first explained to me, I thought bear hunting meant tossing a bag of sweet rolls in the brush and showing up on opening day to bag a bear. Naturally, Dad had different ideas. "We gotta have these baits remote, that way we won't be bothered by other hunters," he said.

"These baits?" I exclaimed. "What do you mean 'these baits?' You said we were both going to hunt over the same bait."

"We are," he answered, "but we can't depend on just one bait. The bears might quit feeding on it for one reason or another. We need a backup bait. Anyway, I asked Bill and David to hunt with us and they'll help us haul the bait."

So there would be four of us. That meant several different bait locations at least.

I could see it happening. What had started as a little bear hunt now showed all the signs of becoming a major expedition. That's Dad for you, everything the hard way.

In the past, we have taken "little walks" that would challenge the endurance of a marathoner. Once, we took "a little portage into Lost Lake" and spent hours trudging in circles through the brush, hauling tons of camping and fishing equipment, not to mention enough food to feed a starving regiment before we found "Lost Lake." Another time, we picked "a few apples for bear bait" and, while hauling them home, were stopped by the state police for exceeding our pickup's two thousand pound load-carrying capacity.

Even with these prior experiences stored close to the surface of my memory, I wanted to hunt bear. So David and I helped Dad and Bill all summer, hauling bait into several sites. Today, we were making our next to the last bait-hauling trip before the start of the season.

We reached the first bait after a two-mile hike. Although I didn't agree with Dad that the bait had to be remote, I had to admit that our bait stations looked good. In fact, they looked so good that just seeing all that bear sign, made the hair stand up on the back of my neck.

There were at least four or five heavily used trails coming into each site and large piles of bear scat everywhere. Careful examination of the trails revealed the tracks of several different bears and one very large track in particular. It looked to me like getting a bear would be a cinch.

After dumping the bait, Dad decided that we should take a seldom-used shortcut back to the cabin. I rolled my eyes and groaned. In the first place, I wasn't too wild about roaming around in the brush with all those bears around. Secondly, in the past, some of his shortcuts have gotten us home several hours after dark.

Luck was with us that day as Bill managed to convince him that taking a shortcut would further spread our scent around and that it was too hot to do any extra walking on the odd chance we went astray.

Bear season would open in three days. We planned to leave home as soon as I was out of school on Friday and meet Bill and David at the cabin. By Friday, I was so excited it was impossible to concentrate in school. When the last bell rang, I left the building like I was shot from a cannon. Dad was packed and ready to leave as soon as I got home.

After the forty-five mile drive, we met Bill and David at the cabin. After talking it over, Bill and Dad decided we had just enough daylight remaining to haul bait into each site one final time. I wasn't wild about the idea. It was late, there was always a chance we could get lost and thanks to all the baiting we had been doing, there were bears roaming around all over the place. It would be just our luck to run into one that might decide to eat the bait out of the pack while it was on our backs rather than waiting until we dumped it. Regardless, Dad and Bill had decided to haul the bait and that was the end of the discussion.

The afternoon was warm and still. The air was heavy and the brush seemed darker and thicker than usual. As far as I was concerned, we couldn't get this bait-hauling chore over fast enough.

We walked from site to site, dropping about a peck of pastry at each one. The bears had eaten every scrap of food we had previously left. It appeared certain we would see bruins the following day.

The last site we went to was one of our best sites. It was also the site my dad and I would hunt the next day.

There was a bend in the trail, just before the bait site and we usually stopped and listened before walking around it, hoping that any bear at the bait would hear us and run off. We didn't want to surprise a bear at close range.

We approached the bend carefully, stopping and listening intently for any sound. It was completely silent, nothing stirred, not even a breath of air. All of a sudden, David let go with a loud belch! My dad and Bill just about jumped out of their pants. Personally, I was pretty sure I was going to have to change my underwear when we got back to the cabin.

"Why the heck did you do that?" my dad exclaimed. "I nearly had a heart attack."

"I'm sorry," David explained, "I couldn't help it."

"Jeez, next time give me a little warning, I nearly died of fright."

It was getting late when we finished the baiting and returned to the cabin. I was about to suggest going to town for a pizza when Dad announced he would do the cooking. Having been a victim of my dad's cooking in the past, I had a sudden loss of appetite. I glanced at David, who didn't look very happy either; I think he was having flashbacks of last deer season when Dad had cooked duck. That meal of duck was pretty bad.

Suspiciously, I asked, "What are we having?"

"Duck," he answered.

"Duck?" Bill questioned.

I glanced at Bill, who looked as though he'd just swallowed something vile. No doubt he also remembered the duck Dad had cooked last deer season.

That was surprising because Bill will eat almost anything that isn't nailed down. That duck from last deer season must have been really bad.

David's reaction was similar. "Duck!" he cried in alarm. "I hate du . . ." he faltered, upon receiving a withering glare from his father.

I'm not wild about duck either but I was beginning to find some humor in the situation. After all, Dad was a duck hunter. Over the years, I'd managed to develop a tolerance for duck. David, on the other hand, thought duck tasted like liver, only worse. Bill is too polite to complain about camp cooking regardless of what is on the menu and he expected David to be the same. It appeared that David was trapped.

We sat down to eat, David and Bill more reluctantly than Dad and I. David tentatively cut a small piece of duck and slowly placed it in his mouth. Dad dove at his plate like a starving coyote. "Great stuff!" he gasped between mouthfuls.

OUTDOOR FOLLIES

Watching Dad slop up that foul-tasting meat was too much for David. He turned green, jumped from the table and headed for the outhouse.

"What's the matter with David?" Dad asked, "Is he sick?"

"Probably just the excitement of the hunt," Bill answered, looking glumly at his plate.

"Well," Dad said, "if he's sick, it's just as well he doesn't eat too much tonight. We don't need to worry about wasting the duck though, we can have it for sandwiches tomorrow."

"Gee, that's a great idea," I thought.

Because bears are more active in the evening, we spent the next morning cleaning up the camp and cutting firewood for the upcoming deer season.

Early September is a pleasant time in northern Wisconsin. The mornings and evenings are cool but daytime temperatures are warm. The sky is usually clear and the leaves are starting to change into a brilliant golden color. It's a great time of the year to be outdoors.

We left the camp at 3:00 p.m. and headed to our respective baits.

Nearing the bait, we approached with caution . . . one careful step at a time. We paused to look and listen. Nothing stirred.

We arrived at the bait and found that all of the bait we had placed the evening before was gone. We dumped a sack of pastry and proceeded to climb into our stands. Our portable tree stands were side by side, twenty feet high, in a white spruce that was located about twenty-five yards from the bait. Once I was seated in the stand, I looked down. Things looked different from up in the tree than they had from the ground. The brush was thick, mostly alder, birch, aspen and spruce. The leaves were still on the trees and visibility in all directions was no more than twenty-five yards.

It was warm and dead-still in the woods. I was comfortable . . . for the first half hour that is; then I started getting fidgety. Every time I moved, I received an evil look from my dad, who somehow was able to remain still. I tried to remain still but this was taking forever. We waited but nothing came to the bait.

The shadows were lengthening as evening drew near. The sun

started to drop below the horizon and it got positively spooky in the woods. Then I heard a sound!

"Did you hear that?" I asked Dad in a voice that was louder than I had intended.

"Yes," he hissed, "get ready, I think a bear is coming."

Just then a bear stepped into the open. He looked huge, at least six feet long with broad, powerful shoulders and a deep chest. He was jet black except for a patch of white on his chest. My heart was pounding so fast that I thought it might explode.

Later, I realized that because the bear was standing broadside about twenty yards from us, he presented a classic opportunity for a chest shot. Yet, at the time, I was struck dumb by the sight of my first black bear in the wild and instead of shooting, I stared wide-eyed.

He stood there like he owned the place, staring at the bait and occasionally lifting his head to sniff the air for signs of trouble. He appeared calm but I had the feeling that if angered, he'd be anything but calm. I was beginning to wonder if shooting a bear was such a great idea after all.

Meanwhile, Dad, realizing I was passing up an opportunity for a perfect shot, was about to go into orbit. Finally, his patience ran out. Risking frightening the bear, he slowly turned to me and mouthed the word, "SHOOT!"

Too late! Just as I was about to shoot, the bear turned, walked to the bait and started to eat. Now he was no longer broadside but stood facing us and I didn't have a decent shot. I glanced at Dad and his look told me to wait. I hoped I didn't have to wait too long as I had already put the gun to my shoulder and it was getting heavy, I didn't know how much longer I could hold it up.

For no apparent reason, the bear suddenly lifted his head, turned broadside and began sniffing the air. This was my chance . . . it was now or never. I picked a spot about five inches behind his shoulder, held the gun as steady as I could and fired.

The bear's reaction was immediate. With lightning speed he jumped into the air, spun around, snarled and ran into a spruce thicket about fifteen yards away. He was so fast that he appeared to be nothing but a black streak. The timber was so dense that we couldn't see him but could hear him tearing up the brush. After a few minutes we couldn't hear him any longer, but since we hadn't heard him run off, we knew he was still in the same location.

For several minutes, we didn't hear anything. My hair, which had been standing on end, was beginning to return to its normal position when we heard a loud growl from the brush into which the bear had run. My hair did an about-face! I looked at Dad, who hadn't spoken a word since I shot. He was about to speak, when he was cut off by another growl from the bear.

"Where the heck did you hit him?" he asked.

"Right where you told me to, just behind the front shoulder," I answered.

He gave me the "I'm not convinced" look and we continued to wait.

After fifteen minutes, during which time we never heard any sounds from the bear, Dad said, "He must be dead. To be on the safe side, let's go back to the cabin and get Bill and David. We'll need them to help get the bear out anyway."

He looked at me and added, "Bob, you're so excited, I'm afraid you'll fall out of the tree while climbing down. You better tie a rope around your chest and I'll let it out as you climb down. When you get near the bottom of the tree, if you hear any sound from the bear, climb back up. Meanwhile, I'll cover you."

"You can junk that idea!" I said, "I ain't getting out of this tree until I know that bear is dead! You go down first."

Dad could tell that I wasn't going to argue the point, so he started down the tree. When he got near the bottom, he yelled in the direction of the bear. There was no response.

"Can you see him?" I asked.

"No. It's too dark under the spruce. I'm positive he's dead. Come on down," he answered.

I started down, ready to scramble back up at any sound from the direction of the bear but nothing stirred.

We didn't waste any time walking back to the cabin where we met Bill and David, told them our story and asked how they had done. Bill explained that they had seen a bear but thought he was too small and decided to pass on him.

After hearing our story, Bill was convinced the bear was dead and suggested that we return with a large plastic sled so we could drag the bear back to the cabin without damaging the hide.

We all headed back to our bait and cautiously crept toward the spot where we had last heard the bear.

"There he is," Bill whispered.

What a beautiful animal! Looking at him filled me with pride and yet, a sense of regret.

He looked bigger on the ground than he had from the tree. His hide was in perfect condition . . . thick, jet black and glossy. When field dressing him, we found that the bullet had hit him exactly where I had aimed.

Then I learned something else about bear hunting. A dead bear can't walk back to the cabin. The bear weighed about two hundred and fifty pounds and was difficult to tie securely to the sled. We'd tie one side and the other would come lose. By the time we were done, we had so many ropes on him that it looked as though we had a net over him. It was a long and difficult drag but we finally got him to the cabin and into the back of Dad's pickup truck.

It's been many years since I shot that bear but I'll never forget the experience. The bear meat has long ago been consumed but I still have vivid memories of that hunt. I also have the bear's skull mounted on a walnut plaque, which Bill boiled and bleached and presented to me as a gift.

Over the years my dad and I have had many great outdoor adventures, like the time a wolverine followed me up a tree or the time we ended up returning to shore in a boat after what had started out as a Lake Superior ice fishing trip. Regardless, that bear hunting trip at Camp Orienta was one of the best.

I'm older now, college is just around the corner. After that, who knows what? One thing is for certain, I'll continue to accompany Dad on outdoor trips, even though I think some of his schemes are crazy. Who knows, perhaps in the future I can come up with a few crazy schemes of my own.

THE TWO HUNDRED DOLLAR FISH FRY

•••••••••••••••••••

A few years ago during our Wisconsin deer season, I returned to the cabin at Camp Orienta after hunting all day. My friend, Jim, was sitting at the table.

"How'd your hunt go?" he asked.

"I didn't shoot a buck if that's what you mean," I replied, "how about you?"

"Good, I shot a nice buck."

"No kidding," I said, surprised, "what time did you get it?"

"Early this afternoon. I went to my stand about 3:00 p.m. and got the deer about ten minutes later."

"It's 5:00 p.m. now. Where's the deer? Why didn't you drag it back to the cabin if you shot it at 3:00 p.m.? You look like you just got here. It only takes fifteen minutes to walk from your stand to the cabin. What took you so long?" I asked.

"What is this? Twenty questions? The deer is right by my stand. We have to go and get it. How do you know I just got back? I might have been back here for a couple of hours already," he said.

"Because you still have your jacket on and you're all sweated up, plus, you're still sober," I answered.

"Ha! And another thing, I'd like to see you walk to my stand in fifteen minutes," he said.

"You're right," I agreed, "It would only take me ten minutes. Let's go, I'll help you drag the deer back to the cabin."

Later, after asking a few questions, I figured out what must have happened.

Jim shot the buck shortly after 3:00 p.m. in the afternoon. The deer ran about forty yards into some thick brush. When Jim got to the location where the deer was standing when he shot at it, he wasn't certain in which direction it ran. As luck would have it, he looked in the wrong direction. Once he was out of sight of his stand, he got turned around. Then, he couldn't find his way back to his stand, even with a compass because he didn't know what direction he had taken when he left the stand. After circling around for an hour and becoming even more confused, he was forced to walk out to the main road, then to the cabin and finally back to his stand, a distance of three miles. Upon arriving back at his stand, he looked in the direction the deer had actually taken and found it dead, eighty yards from where he shot at it.

Of course, Jim has never agreed that this is what happened but I've known him for forty years. As soon as he told me he didn't find the deer right away, I didn't need to be Sherlock Holmes to figure out what happened. What else could explain how he spent three hours looking for a deer that ran eighty yards and died?

"You got lost, didn't you? That's why it took you so long," I said.

"I wasn't lost. I was looking for the deer. Anyway, I had another problem, I lost my knife and I had to walk all the way back to the cabin to get another one," he said.

"You walked back to the cabin after you found the deer? Wow! You did put on a few miles didn't you? How did you manage to forget your knife?" I asked.

"I didn't say I forgot it. I lost it. When I found the deer, I used my knife to cut out the date on the tag, then I put the knife down and moved the deer about ten feet to an open area where it would be easier to gut it. When I went back to get my knife, I couldn't find it. I looked everywhere but I must have lost it in the snow, so I had to go back to the camp for another one," he replied.

"Where did you get another knife?" I inquired.

"I borrowed it from that bag of stuff you have in your truck. You know, the one where you keep your GPS, tree steps, extra gloves and compass. By the way, it looks exactly like the knife I lost last year. I must have left it at the cabin and you found it," he answered.

"You're crazy, that's my knife. Where is it now?"

"Me, crazy? You're the one who's crazy! Anyway, I put the knife down somewhere in the cabin. It's around here someplace. Come on, let's go and get that deer before it gets too dark. I'll find the knife as soon as we get back," he promised.

It actually was his knife. He did leave it at the cabin last year. I picked it up for him and meant to give it back but I forgot. This wasn't the first time that something got lost.

One season my son purchased two new "walkie-talkie" radios. Jim and I were hunting in two stands located about a half mile apart and had planned to hunt until dark. I gave Jim one of the radios and asked him to turn it on after he left his stand so we could keep in touch in case one of us needed help with a deer.

After dark, I called him on the radio. He answered and we agreed to keep the radios on during the remainder of our walk back to the truck. When I met Jim at the truck, I asked him for the radio. He reached in his pocket but the radio was gone.

"I can't find the radio!" he exclaimed.

"You're kidding me. You lost Bob's radio? You used it ten minutes ago, how could you have lost it?" I asked.

"I didn't lose it. I know right where it is," he replied.

"What do you mean, 'you didn't lose it?' If you didn't lose it, where is it?"

"By definition, losing something means you don't know where it is. Since I know where the radio is, I haven't lost it," he explained.

"All right then, where is it?"

"Right along the trail I used coming out of the woods, where it fell out of my pocket. All we have to do is walk back along that trail and we'll find the radio," he answered.

Fortunately, there was snow on the ground so we were able to follow his tracks using our flashlights but we couldn't find the radio. It must have gotten buried in the snow when it fell.

"It should be right around here," Jim said. "I wasn't very far from here when I called you."

"Now can we consider it lost?" I wisecracked.

"Actually, no. Give me the other radio," he asked.

"Why? So you can lose both of them?"

"Just give me the radio and keep quiet. You lose more stuff than I do."

I handed him the radio, curious about why he wanted it.

He took the radio and switched it on. Then he pressed the transmitter and said, "Hey radio, where are you?"

Sure enough, we heard a muffled response from the other radio just in front of us. The radio was on when Jim dropped it and by listening to his transmission, we were able to locate it even though it was buried under the snow.

On the way back to town, I mentioned to Jim that he has been turned around often in the woods.

"Gee, that's funny. I was just about to say the same thing about you," he answered.

Ignoring him, I went on. "That fiasco with you and Mike when we were kids is a prime example," I reminded him.

"I wasn't lost; Mike was," he replied defiantly.

The incident I was referring to happened many years ago, when we were in our early twenties. In those days, Wisconsin didn't have a regular bear season. Bears were only legal game during the nine-day deer season. The only license required was a deer hunting license.

Jim, his cousin, Mike, and I were hunting in a remote wilderness east of Ashland, Wisconsin. We drove out together but were hunting separately. During the course of the morning, Mike and Jim bumped into each other.

They were standing on the edge of a huge ravine, talking about the morning's hunt, when they heard some noise. Looking up, they spotted a black bear walking directly toward them. Without discussing the issue, they both raised their rifles and fired simultaneously at the bear. The bear spun around and ran downhill, expiring next to the creek in the ravine bottom.

It was a big bear. We found out later that it dressed out at two hundred and sixty-two pounds. In Wisconsin, big game cannot be quartered in the field, so getting this bear out of the woods was no laughing matter, especially since it was in the bottom of a large ravine.

It was at least a half mile from the bottom to the top of the ravine, so it was going to be a job to drag the bear out of that hole. Regardless, they were young and enthusiastic and they started dragging the bear up the side of the ravine.

About two hours later, I happened to cross their tracks. I starting following their trail, hoping to catch up to them and find out if they got anything.

Walking up to them, I could see that they were both flushed, sweating profusely and exhausted. "We got a big bear," Jim said, "dragging him out of this ravine nearly killed us."

"What's the story?" I asked.

"We were on the other side of the ravine when the bear walked up to us. After we shot, he ran to the bottom of the ravine and died. You're not gonna believe this but we dragged him all the way to the top on the other side before figuring out that we were dragging him the wrong way. Then we had to drag him back to the bottom and up this side. It was a man killer, I'll never shoot another bear."

"Well, I hope you got a little life left in you because I got some bad news for you. You were dragging him in the right direction in the first place, now you're headed in the wrong direction. The way to the truck is on the other side of the ravine. You're dragging that bear farther into the woods."

"Oh my, God! You can't be right, tell me you're kidding me, please," he gasped.

"Sorry. I'm not guessing either, I'm positive," I said.

"No, I don't believe it! I'll die if I have to drag this bear across this ravine again," he moaned.

"How did you manage to get screwed up? You were going in the right direction at first. Did it ever occur to you to look at your compass?" I asked.

"We forgot to take a compass bearing when we left the road. I crossed so many ravines this morning that I had no idea where we were. We thought we were going in the right direction when we dragged the bear up the other side of the ravine but when we got to the top, we stopped because we weren't one hundred percent certain it was the right direction. After talking it over, we decided we were going the wrong way and reversed direction."

"Well, we better get started dragging. It won't be as bad, I'll help you get him to the top of the other side, then you'll only be about a half mile from the truck," I said, as I picked up the rope and started dragging the bear back down the hill.

Now, many years later, as we were driving home after finding the radio that Jim didn't lose, he agreed.

"Yeah, dragging that bear in the wrong direction was a nightmare all right. I thought we were going in the wrong direction all along but Mike talked me out of it. Regardless, that screwup you made when you nearly got us killed on Lake Superior was a heck of a lot worse than any I've ever made."

I hadn't forgotten about that little incident on Lake Superior either. It happened twenty years ago.

I'd heard a wild rumor in town that other fishermen were catching nice brook trout near the north end of Madeline Island. They all had big, powerful boats but all I owned was a fourteen-foot aluminum boat with an eighteen-horsepower motor. Some would say that such a rig is a little light for Lake Superior, suicidal even, but I figured we could make it if we hit the perfect time on the perfect day.

I gave Jim a call and he agreed to go with me. That alone is all the argument I need to prove that he's crazy. His job was to talk me out of going, instead, he thought it was a good idea. Some friend.

Madeline Island, one of the Apostle Islands, is located near the small town of Bayfield, Wisconsin. We planned to launch our boat in Bayfield and motor to the north end of the island, a distance of thirteen miles. This is a big expanse of water with depths over two hundred feet and long distances between islands. It doesn't take much wind to kick up a heavy sea. We'd be OK if we were careful, furthermore, we could always pull the boat up on an island if we got in trouble. To be on the safe side, I carried an extra tank of gas.

The sky was overcast and the Lake was calm on the morning we launched our boat.

OUTDOOR FOLLIES

"I think we'll be OK," I said.

"Gee, I don't know, Pete, what if the wind picks up?"

"Aw, don't be such a wimp. I doubt if the wind will pick up. If it does, we'll just pull the boat up on Madeline Island until it goes down," I answered.

"All right."

It was dead calm and we motored to the north end of the Island without incident. There were a lot of brook trout there but they were small. Regardless, we fished for a couple of hours before heading back to Bayfield.

On the way back, fog started to rise. I wasn't concerned about it but to be on the safe side, I stayed close to Madeline Island, planning to make the three-mile run to the mainland when we were straight across from Bayfield, rather than cutting across at an angle.

As I made the turn toward Bayfield, the fog got thicker and visibility was reduced to a quarter mile. I wasn't concerned because I could still see the high hills on the mainland above the fog, so I knew I was going in the right direction. About halfway across to Bayfield, the fog closed in completely, reducing visibility to near zero. Now I was worried. I kept motoring in what I thought was the right direction, hoping that at any second we would see Bayfield, but it never happened. After running several more miles, I knew we were hopelessly lost and I stopped to talk it over with Jim.

"I don't know where we are but we should have hit the mainland by now," I said.

"Jeez," Jim said, "I was afraid that something like this would happen. We better use a compass and see if we can follow a straight line."

"That's a good plan," I agreed, "give me your compass."

"Compass? I don't have a compass. This is your boat, where's your compass?" he inquired with a hint of panic in his voice.

"I forgot it," I admitted.

"You forgot it! You dragged me out here in the middle of Lake Superior and you didn't bring a compass? I knew you were going to get me killed one of these days. What an idiot! Now we're in real trouble. For all we know we're halfway to Canada!"

"Hey, I don't remember dragging you into the boat. You should have remembered your own compass. It's just as much your fault as it is mine. Anyway, name calling is not going to help. It's a good thing I brought this extra tank of gas. I'm going to keep running and try to stay on a straight course."

We continued running, hoping we were going in a straight line but after I ran the tank dry without seeing land, it was clear that we weren't. I switched to the other tank and we continued running. It seemed like we ran forever. When the other tank was half empty, I knew we had gone at least twelve miles; but in what direction? Perhaps we should stop and wait for the fog to lift? If we kept running without knowing where we were going, we might run out of gas miles from shore and not have enough to get back when the fog lifted and we could see land.

Suddenly, the wind started to blow. It started with a light breeze but as is typical on Lake Superior, it wasn't long before the wind blew harder.

One good thing about the wind was that now we could follow the direction of the waves and be assured that we were running in a straight line. The temperature had dropped several degrees, which usually means a northeast wind on Lake Superior. With the northeast wind on our backs, we should hit the mainland eventually, depending on where we were and whether or not we had enough gas.

As the wind picked up, the seas got so high that I had to cut the speed to a crawl. We were cold, miserable and frightened. To make matters worse, we were getting seriously low on gas.

"This time you've done it, Pete. We're going to run out of gas and when we do, we'll be broadside to the waves and capsize. We're screwed!" Jim wailed.

I didn't say anything; I was too scared. He was right; because of my foolishness, we were in a desperate situation. I had ventured out on the lake unprepared and had underestimated the weather. Lake Superior is unforgiving.

I'd been in a lot of rough water with my little fourteen-foot boat but these waves were as big as any I had experienced before. Although I had committed a mountain of sins in my short life, this seemed like a good time to dig back into my Catholic past and resurrect a few forgotten prayers.

I picked up the gas tank and shook it. Not much left, less than a gallon.

"Jim, we're almost out of gas. Let's put the oars in the oarlocks so when we run out of gas, we can use them to try and keep the boat from getting sideways in the waves and capsizing. You might also want to think about praying."

"Think about praying? Let me tell you what I'm thinking about. I'm thinking about murder!"

"Then I won't be able to help you row."

"It would be worth it. We're going to drown anyway!"

We got the oars ready and continued to motor along at a snail's pace.

The wind was dispersing the fog and visibility was starting to improve, when suddenly, incredibly, I thought I could see land.

"Jim! Look! I think I see land."

He looked in the same direction I was looking. "Yes, I see it too," he answered excitedly. "It must be one of the islands. Thank God! We'll find a place to pull the boat up and wait until somebody comes by. We might be able to bum some gas or at least they can call the Coast Guard."

The Apostle Islands are remote. It could be a day or more before somebody came by but it was better than the alternative. I worked my way slowly toward shore, looking for a place where we could beach the boat.

As we got closer, I noticed that there were power poles along the shoreline about one hundred yards inland. That meant we had found the mainland or Madeline Island because all of the other islands are completely undeveloped and had no power poles. I had no idea where we were because I couldn't remember any place on Madeline Island or the mainland where power poles were visible near shore.

"Jim," I exclaimed, "we're going to be all right. I don't know where we are and I don't care, we're beaching the boat."

I could see waves breaking on a sand beach and headed toward it. My boat is fairly light and if we were careful, we could run to shore on top of a wave and pull it up without taking any water over the transom.

It worked perfectly. We came in on a wave, timed our jump from the boat exactly and pulled the boat up high and dry before the next wave crashed down. Scrambling, we dragged the boat another fifty yards inland. We'd made it!

The power poles that we saw from the lake ran along a road. We walked to the road and saw a man jogging toward us.

"Where did you guys come from?" he asked. "What were you doing out there in that little boat? You're lucky to be alive. Are you crazy?"

"I'm not, but my friend is," Jim said in a deadpan voice.

We explained what happened and asked where we were. I wouldn't have been surprised if he said Isle Royale.

"You're at Big Bay, on the south side of Madeline Island," he answered.

"Big Bay? You're kidding." That meant we had motored completely around the Island, which is thirteen miles long, and somehow missed the other Apostle Islands in the process. It was incredible but true.

The fog continued to lift and visibility kept improving but it was too rough to consider getting gas and trying to run the boat back to Bayfield. Our only solution was to call our wives, ask them to pick up my truck and trailer in Bayfield, then take the car ferry from Bayfield to Madeline Island and pick us up.

Our new friend gave us a ride to LaPointe, the only village on the Island. I called my wife and explained what happened. She wasn't too wild about all the monkey business involved in getting my truck and coming across on the ferry but agreed to do it nonetheless. She said she would pick up Jim's wife and they would meet us in LaPointe at the ferry dock. She also thought that it would be nice if Jim and I took them out for dinner on the Island for all the trouble they were going through. That was fine with me, I just wanted to get my boat and motor home without drowning. It was Friday, we could probably find a fish fry at one of the Island restaurants.

After asking around, we found that there were only two restau-

OUTDOOR FOLLIES

rants on the island.

Nothing on Madeline Island is cheap but one restaurant had the reputation of good food at reasonable prices, while the other, a prestigious Island restaurant called "The Club House," offered gourmet food at higher prices. We opted for the lower-priced restaurant and walked over there to have a beer while we waited. When we got there, we found out that because of a recent kitchen fire, they weren't serving meals. The bartender told us that if we wanted to eat at The Club House, we'd better make reservations. I called for a reservation and asked about a fish fry.

"Fish fry?" the person who took our reservations sniffed. "Of course we serve fish but I'd hardly call it a 'fish fry.'"

"Well," I answered, "whatever you call it, we're going to have it. Can I make a reservation for 6:00 p.m.?"

"Of course sir, how many in your party?"

I could tell by the uppity tone of his voice that this wasn't going to be a cheap meal. I was used to spending about three bucks for a fish fry but I figured, "What the heck, it doesn't hurt to splurge once in a while, so what if it cost me a couple bucks more?"

It was three hours before we were due to meet our wives and we spent the entire time in the bar. By the time they got to the Island, we'd had enough to drink.

Madeline Island is a sailboat mecca, frequented by wealthy Minneapolis and St. Paul people in town for a weekend of sailing. The Club House was very upscale and filled with patrons in natty sailing attire. I call them "the beautiful people." Our wives were dressed for dinner but Jim and I wore nothing but our fishing clothing. We raised a few eyebrows as we were escorted to our table, one of which belonged to the hostess who seated us.

I opened the menu and nearly collapsed! "Look at the prices!" I gasped. "Everything's separate . . . the entrée, the salad and soup. Look, twenty-six dollars for a steak, six dollars for a salad, it's highway robbery!"

"Pete," my wife hissed, "be quiet, you're embarrassing me. Don't make such a fuss, we can afford to do this once."

I'd seen that look before and I knew it was time to quit complaining and make the most of it. We ordered drinks, wine, appetizers and dinner. You'd think we were millionaires.

When we were finished, I'd had enough to drink to forget that money was a factor in my life and was into the spirit of the occasion. "Here we are," I said, "after a harrowing experience, having dinner with our wives, surrounded by the beautiful people. What more could we ask for?"

"How about the bill?" Jim said.

I got the waiter's attention and asked for the bill. When I saw it, I nearly choked! One hundred and ninety-six dollars! After my generous tip, an even two hundred, at a time when gas was thirty-six cents a gallon! It was my first and last two hundred dollar fish fry!

Yes, I had to admit that neither Jim nor I had an edge on getting lost. We're both forgetful and have spent plenty of time trying to find our way out of the woods.

Still, there was another incident that would prove that he's more forgetful than I, but I can't remember what it was.

UNCLE TOM

• • • • • • • • • • •

As a result of centuries-old glacial activity, Wisconsin has a narrow band of sand hills that stretch from midwestern Wisconsin all the way north across the Bayfield Peninsula to Lake Superior. Those sand hills located on the Bayfield Peninsula are known as "The Barrens" and almost all are included in the Chequamegon National Forest.

In addition to providing excellent wildlife habitat for a variety of birds and animals in the Lake Superior Basin, these sand hills also contain the perfect soil mixture needed for growing wild blueberries. In fact, Iron River, Wisconsin, which is located on the southern boundary of The Barrens, considers itself the "Blueberry Capital of the World" and has an annual "Blueberry Festival."

The amount of blueberries found each year varies, depending on the weather. Some years they are plentiful and other years there are none, but usually there are a few good patches scattered around.

Finding and picking blueberries is a popular summertime activity for many of the northern Wisconsin residents. Almost everybody picks a few blueberries, especially when they're plentiful, but for some people, it's a passion. You'd think the berries were made of gold. They will spend hours hunting for them, rarely divulge their location to anybody and go through great lengths to deceive others in hopes of keeping "their patch" to themselves.

I have such a passion. If I find a good patch of blueberries in a year when they're hard to find, I only divulge the location to a few select friends, usually after I've picked most of the berries and only then because I have ulterior motives.

Here's my rationale. If I tell somebody about the berries I've found, they will quit looking for berries on their own and will pick my patch dry. Therefore, not only will they fail to become a potential source of blueberry information for me, but also will fill their freezers with my berries. On the other hand, if I never tell anybody where I've found blueberries, nobody will ever tell me about the berries they've found.

Here's a plan I've used a time or two. When the patch you have been picking is starting to run dry and you have a friend whom you suspect has been finding berries elsewhere but not telling you about them, offer to take him with you to pick berries in your patch. He may refuse but it's far more likely that greed will take over and he will reason that he can always go back to his patch after he cleans yours out. When you both arrive at your patch and see that the berries have been mostly picked already, you can say, "Jeez, I was here just two days ago and there were a lot more berries. I guess it doesn't pay to pick here, do you know a place where we can look?" You won't be lying either, because there were more berries two days ago, no doubt the birds and mice ate some berries. Then, when he takes you to his patch, you can spend the next several days picking it clean. Caution! Do not attempt this ruse more than once on the same person, especially if he is large and has a history of aggression.

My friend, Bill, has a passion for picking blueberries. He also is good at finding them when they are scarce; perhaps even better than I am, because he can actually remember the location of a good patch from year to year, while I have trouble finding the patch I picked in the day before. He's tipped me off to a couple of good patches over the years, of course it was only after he had picked most of the berries himself, but I've always appreciated the information and have tried to reciprocate.

Bill's uncle, Tom, a retired Great Lakes boat captain, loves to pick blueberries.

Those of us who know him well call him, "Uncle Tom." He is a great guy but sometimes devious when it comes to blueberries. I don't know how good he is at finding blueberries, because he's never told me about any blueberries he's found, but he has an uncanny ability to find patches of blueberries other people have found. Once he finds your patch, he will camp on it from daylight to dark until

OUTDOOR FOLLIES

the last blueberry is picked.

It's incredible. When I'm not finding any berries, I never see Uncle Tom but when I luck onto a good patch, he will inevitably show up. It's happened too many times to be a coincidence. The man has some sort of sixth sense that enables him to sniff out where you're finding blueberries!

If you happen to find a nice patch of blueberries and Uncle Tom gets wind of it, he will grill you about its location. If you slip up and give him the slightest hint of the general location, he'll hunt you down until he finds you picking in the patch. Then, he won't leave the patch until the last blueberry has been picked. To make it worse, even though he's in his eighties now, he can pick blueberries like a machine.

I was introduced to Uncle Tom nearly twenty years ago, during the first summer after he retired.

That year there were a few berries almost everywhere but not many good patches. I was picking berries in a remote, roadless area north of Iron River, Wisconsin. I didn't know the area very well, so I drove around with my pickup to get a feel for it. It was immense with only a few old grown-up logging roads going into it, none of which appeared safe to drive. I drove as far into the heart of the area as I dared, which wasn't very far, then parked my truck and started to walk.

I walked for what seemed like miles, in fact I wasn't certain I could find my truck again, when suddenly I found a great patch of blueberries. They were everywhere. The ground was blue with them.

A lot of people had been looking for blueberries for weeks already, but this spot hadn't been touched because it was in the middle of nowhere, miles from the nearest road. What luck! The berries were big, in clusters and plentiful.

In twenty minutes I'd already picked four quarts. This patch was a bonanza, it looked like I could pick for days and not run out of berries.

Suddenly, I heard an animal snuffling toward me in the brush. I have a great fear of bears and was startled, thinking a bear was coming after me. I jumped up to defend myself but was surprised to see it was a dog. It looked like a springer spaniel. He ran up to me and began to wag his tail. What the heck was a springer spaniel doing out here in the middle of nowhere? Where did he come from?

It didn't take me long to find out. Right behind the dog, berry pail in hand, walked Uncle Tom. "Oh Boy!" he exclaimed, "this is a nice patch of berries you found. I haven't seen any berries like this all year. Wow, look at all the berries."

"Where the heck did you come from?" I asked.

"I saw your truck. I drove by it twice and since you were gone for over an hour, I figured you had found some berries so I started looking around."

"How did you know where I was?" I inquired.

"It was easy, I just drove in here and saw you," he replied.

"How could you see me? I'm miles from my truck. There's no road near here," I said.

"Sure there is, right over there, about two hundred yards away. That's where I'm parked," he answered.

"I didn't know there was a road there," I said.

"Oh yes," he replied, "the loggers put it in about fifteen years ago when they logged this area. Not a lot of people know about it."

That day was August 1st. Uncle Tom never left that patch. Later that fall, he admitted to me that he picked berries in the same general area until the first frost in September. If there's a berry left, Uncle Tom will find it.

Several years later, during another year when we had a sparse berry crop, I found a patch late in the season. I picked about fifteen quarts but had to quit because it was getting dark. There were plenty of berries left but I was leaving on a business trip that would keep me out of the area for two weeks and I knew the berries would be spoiled by the time I got back, therefore, I called Bill and Uncle Tom and told them the location of the patch.

I didn't realize it at the time but I nearly touched off a family feud. It turned out that Bill had to work the next day but since Uncle Tom was retired, he was free.

OUTDOOR FOLLIES

"I get off work at three tomorrow afternoon," Bill said to Uncle Tom, "I'll pick you up and we'll go out there together."

"Oh. . . I don't know," Tom said, "I'd like to go out a little earlier."

"Yeah, so you can get at those blueberries before me. Forget it, you can wait until I get off work," Bill repeated.

"OK," Tom agreed, "but I want to take my own truck out there because I might not want to stay as late as you. I'll leave town at three o'clock and meet you there."

"Alright," Bill agreed.

Uncle Tom woke up the next morning and found that the day was cool with a clear blue sky. It was a perfect day for picking berries and he couldn't get that blueberry patch out of his mind. "Perhaps Bill wouldn't mind if I went out just a little earlier than we had planned," he thought. "What difference would an hour or so make? That wouldn't hurt anything, would it? After all, I'm nearly eighty years old, shouldn't I get a little head start on my younger nephew? Didn't I work summers for forty years on the Great Lakes ore boats while others, including Bill, picked blueberries? I should be entitled to a break now and then, shouldn't I?" The more he thought about it, the more he justified it in his mind.

As the pressure mounted, his resolve weakened until he gave in, which happened approximately two minutes after the idea first occurred to him. He decided to drive out there, look the patch over, find out how big it was and where the best picking would be. "There's nothing wrong with that," he thought, "I'll be doing Bill a favor."

When Bill arrived, Uncle Tom had already picked fifteen quarts.

"Thanks for waiting for me," Bill said.

"I just got here a little while ago," Tom replied.

"Well, then you're a pretty fast picker," Bill said, "this patch looks like a herd of buffalo ran through it."

"Oh, there are plenty of berries left, you'll never pick them all," Tom answered sheepishly.

There were plenty of berries left and Bill didn't want to make his uncle feel bad, so he dropped the subject and started picking berries. Regardless, Bill never forgot the incident and he and I have had a good laugh over it more than once. Also, for the next several years, Bill was pretty slow to tip Uncle Tom off to any berry patches.

I ran into Uncle Tom a couple years later and asked if he was finding any berries. "Yeah, I got a few but not many," he answered.

"Gee, that's funny," I said. "I was talking to Bill and he said he was getting lots of berries."

"Yeah," Uncle Tom grumbled, "he'll tell everybody else where to go but he won't tell me until the patch is nearly all picked."

"Can you blame him?" I laughed. "If he told you, every berry in the patch would be in your freezer."

"Harrumph!" he grunted.

During the summer after my retirement, blueberries were scarce. I found very few and heard from other people that they weren't finding many either. Regardless, since I was retired I had plenty of extra time so I kept looking.

After several weeks of looking and finding very few berries, I was about to give up. Then, in a last ditch effort, I decided to drive into an area where I'd only found berries once before. The road into the area was nothing but a snake trail of loose sand and rocks and I needed four-wheel drive to claw my way into it. It was a huge area and I had no idea where to look, so I parked my truck at random and started walking.

I walked several miles in a big circle. It was hot and dry and I found very few berries. After a couple of hours, I was working my way back to my truck, which was still about a half mile away, when I came to the base of a high hill. I had already given up any hope of finding any blueberries but I was still curious about what I might find over the top of that hill. After thinking it over, I decided that before I gave up, I'd walk up and over that big hill to take a look, even though it would take me farther away from my truck.

As I started nearing the top, I found a few berries. When I crested the hill, I hit the mother lode. It was full of berries. They had been shaded from the sun by the brush and ferns and were big, blue

OUTDOOR FOLLIES

and grew in clumps. I couldn't believe my luck to find these berries after having walked for miles without finding any.

It was already late in the day and I only had time to pick one bucket. I filled my pail in no time and returned to my pickup, planning to be back out there the next morning.

That evening, I attended church services. Uncle Tom, a member of our church, was also at church that evening.

At eighty-five, thanks to a lifetime of hard work and moderation with food and beverage, Uncle Tom was still in very good physical condition, however his back was his Achilles' heel. He was currently recovering from back surgery, was walking with a cane and had to be seated in a church pew designed for our handicapped parishioners.

In a moment of weakness, I considered telling him about the berries I'd found. But after thinking it over, I decided that because of his handicap, he would not be able to pick any berries anyway, much less walk up a big hill and might feel frustrated about missing out. Therefore, I decided the right thing to do was to say nothing about the berries.

The next day was perfect for picking blueberries: cool, clear and a nice breeze. I arrived at the location early, excited to start picking. It would have been nice to be able to drive a little closer to the patch but there were no roads. There was a power line that came from beyond the berry patch and ran down the hill, across the road and continued on to a substation. I thought about driving up the hill along the power line, but it was so steep and sandy it would have been impossible even with four-wheel drive.

"It's just as well," I thought, "I'll carry water and an extra five-gallon pail for my berries and stay right up there until I'm done. Nobody will have any idea where I am even if they do spot my truck."

I pulled my truck off the road into the brush, so it would be difficult to see if somebody should happen to drive by. It really wasn't necessary as I was wearing a camouflaged shirt and the berries were located almost a mile away, but I wasn't taking any chances.

I climbed that monster hill and found the patch just as I'd left it the day before, full of lush blueberries.

The area had been burned by a forest fire several years earlier and there were many burned logs laying around. Bears had been there, feasting on the blueberries and also had turned over almost every log looking for bugs and ants. I could tell that some of the logs had been turned recently because the grass they were laying on was green and looked as though it had not been crushed very long ago. The new growth in the burned area was thick and so high that I couldn't see over the top. A bear could be right next to me and I'd have no idea he was there. I started getting nervous; I always do when there are bears around. I regretted that I wasn't carrying my pistol but I did have pepper spray with me.

I decided to make noise at regular intervals, so if a bear was poking around or bedded near me, he would hear me and run off. Therefore, as I picked, I sang, yelled and coughed regularly.

The picking was excellent. I was bent over, intent on picking a particularly lush bush full of berries, when I heard a loud growl. "What the hell was that?" I thought as I leaped to my feet, fumbling for my pepper spray. I stood up and with shaking hands got the pepper spray out and pointed the can in the direction from which I heard the growl. I stared intently but because of the thick brush, I couldn't see anything. Then I heard the growl again and I could hear something walking toward me. I was nearly paralyzed with fright and looked around for a tree to climb but there were none. "I wonder if this pepper spray will work?" I thought, remembering that the instructions recommended frequent testing. Deciding to try a little squirt, I pointed the can in the direction the growl had come from and let fly.

The pepper spray worked perfectly, a strong stream ejected from the can as well as a fine mist. Unfortunately, I should have paid closer attention to the wind, because even though I directed the pepper spray away from me, the wind blew it back into my face. Damn! That stuff was bad! It wasn't like having it sprayed directly in my face but it was bad enough. My eyes were burning and I started coughing and sneezing. I momentarily forgot about the bear and dove for the water I'd brought along. Fortunately, I hadn't taken a

OUTDOOR FOLLIES

full blast and was able to wash most of it out of my eyes.

Just then, a man stood up in front of me. I couldn't tell who he was because he had a bug screen over his head but I recognized his voice when he said, "Wow, look at all the blueberries! Look at all the blueberries!"

"Uncle Tom!" I exclaimed, "What the heck are you doing here? You're supposed to be handicapped."

"I am," he replied, " I nearly killed myself walking in here."

"You're a fraud! You sit in the handicapped pew in church! I ought to turn you into the Pope!"

"Ha!" he snorted, "I'm eighty-five years old. I can sit anywhere in church I want to. When you're my age, you'll be lucky if you aren't lying down permanently. By the way, are you afraid of bears? Is that why you were making all that racket? And, what's that smell?"

"That smell is pepper spray, I was testing my can. And yes, I'm afraid of bears and I'm not ashamed to admit it. You should be afraid of them too. By the way, thanks for growling at me. I was so frightened that if I would have had a gun I might have accidentally shot you."

"Pepper spray? The bears like that stuff. Haven't you ever heard how you can tell the difference between cougar scat and bear scat?"

"No," I admitted.

"The bear scat is the stuff with pepper spray in it," he chuckled. "You don't need to be afraid of bears," he continued, "they won't hurt you. I'm glad you are though, because I heard all that noise you were making and that's how I found you. By the way, you have a lousy singing voice. If there was a bear around here, he'd be five miles away by now and still running."

"What are you talking about? You couldn't have heard me from the road, it's too far away," I exclaimed.

"Too far? I'm parked right over there," he gestured, pointing over his shoulder. "Come over here, you can see my truck."

"I didn't know there was a road there," I said, astounded.

"Sure there is. It's not much of a road and you need four-wheel drive to use it but it's a road. I remembered when they put it in here twenty-five years ago, the same time they constructed the power line."

"How did you know to look for me up here?" I asked.

"I saw your truck on the road below us yesterday. Then last night in church, you looked as though you'd been in the sun all day and I wondered if you might have found some blueberries; they're pretty scarce this year you know. Anyway, I figured I'd take a ride out here today and sure enough, I found where you'd pulled off the road and hid your truck. Then, I saw your boot tracks in the sand where you crossed that road and walked up the hill. I looked for you on the hillside with binoculars but couldn't see you, so I figured you were over the top. It was a good thing too because I wouldn't have been able to climb up there anyway. That's when I remembered that old road. I drove around until I found where it split off from the main road and although I nearly got stuck a couple of times, I was able to drive all the way here. I still didn't know where you were but you were making such a commotion, it was easy to find you. Wow! Look at all these blueberries!"

Talk about history repeating itself. Here he was, once again, driving right up to a location that I thought was inaccessible. Well, what are you going to do? The truth is, I was glad to see him and there were plenty of berries for both of us.

I saw Uncle Tom again this summer, two years and another back surgery later. He was picking blueberries in a patch that his nephew, Bill, had found and told us about. It was hotter than blazes, ninety plus degrees and not a breath of wind but there he was, hours on end, picking blueberries. Because of his bad back, he couldn't kneel down and bend his back to pick, so he had to find a good patch and sit down. After he picked all the berries he could reach, he'd move to another spot and sit down. "Tom," I said, "when are you going to give up blueberry picking?"

"Oh, I don't know," he replied wearily, "I suppose when they drag me out of here on a stretcher."

I still see Tom every Saturday evening at church. He still sits in the handicapped section, the old fraud. But it's really good to see him.

WHY I NEVER BECAME A BIG GAME GUIDE

••••••••••••••••••••••

The grizzly we had been watching lifted his head and stared in our direction. I froze but my bow-hunter client moved slightly. The bear saw the movement and without hesitation came for us at full speed with murder in his eyes.

I raised my rifle to my shoulder deciding that if he came within twenty-five yards, I'd shoot. When he crossed the twenty-five yard mark without showing any sign of slowing down, I took careful aim and fired. CLICK! Darn . . . misfired! I'd have to stop loading shells during happy hour.

At that point my client decided it was time to vacate the premises and scrambled up a spruce tree to a height of thirty feet, a remarkable feat given the fact that the tree was only twenty feet tall.

Dropping the rifle, I calmly drew my single shot .44 magnum pistol, took careful aim between his eyes and at a distance of ten feet, I . . . that's when I woke up!

I sat bolt upright in bed trembling with excitement. I decided right then and there to become a big game guide when I graduated from high school the following year.

When I told my father about my plans, I could tell he was impressed by the way he laughed. "What ya gonna do if a grizzly charges you?" he guffawed, continuing to chuckle to himself as he left for work.

"Figures," I thought to myself. My dad rarely took any of my ideas seriously, probably because as I was growing up I'd already decided to be a fireman, police officer, frogman and professional hunter in Africa.

Peter F. Crowley

What my dad didn't know is that growing up in our neighborhood provided many experiences that taught one the skills necessary to avoid a mauling in an animal attack. A good example is what happened during my junior year of high school during football practice.

Our team was participating in an intramural scrimmage. The fullback on one squad, nicknamed "Rhino," was six feet four inches tall, weighed two hundred and forty pounds and had a brain inversely proportional to the size of his body.

It didn't surprise his fellow teammates when he picked up a fumble and ran the wrong way scoring a touchdown for the opposition. Rhino's bad temper was notorious and nobody had the nerve to criticize him for his dumb play... except me of course.

I was not very large or athletic, but I tried to make up for what I lacked in size and ability by being quick with clever comments. I was on the team opposing Rhino and was quick to congratulate him after he had scored for us by saying, "Nice run, Rhino. Clever the way you were able to avoid all those tackles, but didn't you ever wonder why the guys from your own team were trying to tackle you?"

After taking a moment to decipher what I had said, ample time for me and the rest of the team to back away, his face turned red and in a rage he tried to get at me threatening to tear my head off and do something anatomically impossible with it. Fortunately, the coach was able to restrain him, to the dismay of the rest of the team who were standing by with amused detachment expecting to witness a murder.

The next day I was taking a shortcut to school through an alley when I saw Rhino coming from the opposite direction. He spotted me and instantly charged. I was only ten feet from a telephone pole conveniently equipped with climbing steps so I sprang to the pole and climbed to a height of fifteen feet, relieved to see that Rhino apparently had a fear of heights and was unwilling to climb up after me.

I was safe for the moment but Rhino was so infuriated that I thought he might charge the pole itself. Instead, he picked up rocks and began throwing them at me. His aim was poor and the rocks sailed harmlessly past, arching to the ground some distance away but not before striking Joe Gazedske's car, which was parked in his

OUTDOOR FOLLIES

backyard just off the alley.

Joe, a retired truant officer who had spent a lifetime being tormented by truant kids, happened to be hoeing in his garden out of Rhino's sight. Hearing the rocks strike his car he looked our way just in time to see Rhino pick up another rock. Thinking he had finally caught one of his tormentors in the act, Joe charged after Rhino determined to plant the hoe handle firmly between his eyes. Before long, all I could see was a cloud of dust with Rhino leading and Joe in hot pursuit. As soon as they were out of sight, I climbed down from the pole and went merrily on my way.

Another good example is what happened during our school shop class one day. Our teacher, Mr. Grubs, nicknamed "Thumbs," because of the loss of two complete fingers from one hand and parts of fingers from the other, was a notorious grouch. He walked with a peculiar swinging gait, a result of a semi-stiff knee suffered in an accidentally self-inflicted injury from a sledge hammer blow received when he was trying to hit a steel wedge that had become lodged in a block of wood. His face was set in a perpetual scowl, accented by a wildly fluttering "tic" under his left eye, which became worse whenever he was particularly agitated.

Shop class was often boring and to liven things up, I occasionally would play a little prank on Mr. Grubs. I knew that he strongly suspected me of the pranks but thus far I had avoided all but circumstantial evidence.

On the day in question, Mr. Grubs was in a particularly foul mood. His tic was completely out of control and he stormed around the shop grumbling constantly. Thinking the timing was perfect for a prank, I quietly sneaked up behind him and mimicked his every move including his peculiar gait.

Mr. Grubs suspected something was going on because the rest of the class was tied in knots trying to keep from laughing out loud but he couldn't put his finger (I mean thumb) on the problem. I got so absorbed in my performance, I didn't notice a shiny piece of sheet metal leaning against the bench that reflected my every movement. The reflection eventually caught his eye and seeing what I was up to, he turned in a flash and attacked, swinging wildly at me with a crippled right hand. Only my lightning reflexes saved me from a severe mauling as I was able to duck under the blow. Mr. Grubs was no match for me in speed, although he gave a remarkable effort for a sixty-year-old man with a bum leg, but I was able to dart to the safety of the hallway. Running for the front door while looking over my shoulder, I almost collided with our principal, Mr. Squathammer, who stopped me with a nifty open field tackle.

I spent the next several hours in his office until released to the custody of my father who had been called to the school office from work. My father took a rather dim view of my antics and seemed particularly disturbed about being called away from work. I did suffer a verbal mauling that evening.

So, as you can see, I thought I was well prepared for the life of guiding big game hunters in the pursuit of dangerous game. However, an incident that happened shortly thereafter changed my entire outlook.

It started innocently enough when my mother asked me to stop at the home of one of her friends to pick up a skein of yarn she needed to finish a sweater she was knitting.

The friend lived on the outskirts of town in a run-down house. I drove into the driveway and went to the back porch, which was a boxed-in affair with an ill-fitting door. Not wanting to enter unannounced, I knocked rather sharply hoping someone inside the house would hear me. What I didn't notice was a large German shepherd dog sleeping just inside the door. The sharp knock caused the door to swing slowly inward and triggered a reaction by the dog that was just short of spectacular. He leaped to his feet in a snarling rage and came for my throat. My life flashed before my eyes, and for a moment I thought I was a goner but luckily I was able to insert my finger into the hole where the doorknob should have been and pull the door closed. The door was so badly out of alignment that there was an opening of nearly three inches near the bottom. The dog was doing his best to get at me by shoving his snout through that opening. I couldn't take my finger out of the opening because the minute I released the pressure, the door would swing open. Sensing he couldn't force the door open, the dog began tearing chunks of wood from the

OUTDOOR FOLLIES

doorjamb while continuing to snarl and foam at the mouth.

I kept thinking someone from within the house would rescue me but it gradually dawned on me that no one was home.

Spying a broom leaning against the steps, I grabbed it thinking I would poke at the dog and perhaps he would move far enough from the door to give me enough time to make a run for my car. Not a chance! It only proved to further infuriate him.

It was at this point that real panic began to set in. For all I knew, I might spend the rest of my life, which wasn't going to be much longer judging by the way the dog was tearing at the jamb, standing on those steps with my finger in the doorknob hole.

I glanced at the roof thinking I might be able to climb up before the dog could reach me. That's when I spotted a piece of haywire that had been used to hold up the end of a rain gutter. I was saved! All I had to do was unwire the rain gutter and wire the door shut. Holding the door shut with my finger, I used my free hand to unwire the rain gutter. I gingerly slipped the wire through the opening in the door and secured it to the railing.

"Yuk! Yuk! Yuk," I thought smugly to myself. "You gotta get up pretty early in the morning to fool old Pete."

I started for my car but paused at the foot of the stairs, not able to resist one little taunt at the dog. "Ruff! Ruff! Ruff!" I growled in my best dog vocabulary. "Doggy going to miss a meal?" The dog came unhinged! Infuriated because his prey was escaping, he gathered all his strength for one last Herculean lunge at the door. He hit the door with his full force and to my everlasting horror, I watched in shock as the wire broke!

The next few minutes remain cloudy in my memory but in less than two seconds I wet my pants, went from zero to sixty miles per hour and dove into my car slamming the door no more than a hair's breadth in front of the dog's snapping jaws.

That did it. There was no longer any question in my mind; facing dangerous animals was not in my future.

I might have convinced myself that I acted in a cool and courageous manner, but I'd never convince my dad who was doubled up in laughter after witnessing the entire event from the front seat.

CAMP MICE

• • • • • • • • • • • • •

Last week, Bill, Doc and I made our annual spring pilgrimage to Camp Orienta.

When we open the door to the cabin in the spring after the building has been closed all winter, we're never sure what we're going to find. Squirrels, weasels, mice and even birds have occasionally found their way in. But this year, nothing, other than a mouse running across the floor. The camp looked the same as when we left it . . . a mess.

The mouse looked happy to see us, as though we were friends dropping by for a visit. He had apparently forgotten that we were responsible for the demise of forty-three of his relatives the previous fall. I know it was forty-three because I kept a record on the cabin wall.

"Look at that, Bill," I said. "A mouse just ran across the floor. There must be a million of them in here. I thought we had them cleaned out last fall."

"I doubt it. It's hard to get all of them. All they need are a few survivors and a boring winter to build up a new batch by spring. Regardless, they won't hurt anything," Bill replied.

"That's what you say. I'd just as soon that they find another place to live. It's not that I have anything against them, I just don't like sharing my living quarters with them.
They bother me"

"Actually," Doc said, "there are some sound health reasons that support ridding one's living quarters of mice."

"Oh yeah," I answered, "what health reasons?"

"Mice can carry Hanta fever."

"What the heck is Hanta fever?" I inquired.

"Hanta fever is one of the hemorrhagic fevers, part of the same family of diseases as Ebola and Marberg fever. The fever is caused by the Hanta virus which is normally transmitted from a rodent to man. Up north here, that rodent would be the white-footed mouse. In North America, Hanta fever is the most common of the hemorrhagic fevers. It can be quite serious," Doc replied.

"How serious?"

"Deadly. It starts with a fever and flu-like symptoms. In a short time you begin bleeding internally. Without immediate medical treatment you will continue to worsen until you are bleeding out of every orifice of your body. Then, after suffering in agony for six to ten days, you have a fifty percent chance of dying. Unless, of course, you're lucky enough to have me as your physician, in which case I can double your likely lifespan and you will suffer from ten to twenty days, become thirty thousand dollars poorer and still have a fifty percent chance of dying."

"Holy cow," I said, "that's horrible!"

"Yeah," said Bill, "I'd hate to lose thirty thousand dollars."

After hearing about Hanta fever, I wanted to be around mice even less than before. But how can I help it? They're everywhere. They've practically taken over Camp Orienta.

At first we thought we could eliminate them by removing all sources of food but that didn't work. They ate flies. That's right, flies! And one thing Camp Orienta has plenty of are flies. We'd come to the camp after it had been closed up for a few weeks and we'd find thousands of fly wings but no fly bodies. The mice had eaten everything but the wings.

Mice don't bother Bill. In fact, he sees them as camp companions. One year, when we were cleaning up the camp after deer season, we ran out of time and needed to leave before we were finished when Bill said, "Don't worry about the mess; we can leave the camp the way it is."

"If we left a fish camp in Ontario in this condition, we'd lose our deposit," I answered.

"Yeah, I know it, but that's what I like about Camp Orienta, let the mice clean it."

OUTDOOR FOLLIES

The mice know Bill is their friend too. One year, during deer season, I was awakened during the night by some small animal making noise. I tried to ignore it and go back to sleep but it kept making a racket. Finally, I got up and looked around with a flashlight and located the noise, which was being made by a mouse that had jumped into a five-gallon plastic bucket to inspect a candy wrapper and couldn't get out.

When I first put the light on him he wasn't concerned at all. He probably thought I was Bill and he was going to ask for a handout. Then he recognized me and got very nervous, no doubt remembering the fate of his relatives earlier in the fall. He scrambled around in the bottom of the pail, trying to hide under the candy wrapper but he was dead meat and he knew it.

I didn't know what to do with him. I considered filling the pail half full of water but that seemed unnecessarily harsh. "To heck with it," I thought. "He really hasn't hurt anything; I'll just take him outside and dump him out of the pail."

I turned on the yard light, went outside, closed the door and walked about thirty feet from the building. Just as I started to tip the pail, the mouse made a break for it. I couldn't believe my eyes! He made an Olympic-caliber jump from the half-turned pail and ran for the building at Mach speed. Reaching it in a split second, he disappeared through a crack in the siding so narrow that a mosquito would have had trouble squeezing through. Unbelievable! That mouse was out of the pail and back in the building in less than a second. I realized then that he'd probably been in and out of the building a hundred times!

I walked back into the camp and shined the light around. There he was, sitting on Bill's forehead, while Bill was blissfully snoring. I considered clubbing him with a piece of oak firewood but I didn't want to wake up Bill.

Our sauna has mice too. I often wonder what they think when the temperature fluctuates from below zero to two hundred degrees in two hours? It doesn't seem to bother them. You'd think they'd pack up and go to the neighbors where they wouldn't have to put up with such nonsense, but they don't.

We try to trap the mice in a vain attempt to get rid of them, but it doesn't work. There are always more. Making mice is what mice do for recreation. Furthermore, I hate removing them from traps. It doesn't bother Bill though. He can take a mouse out of a trap with his bare hands, fling it out the door and be eating a slice of cheese ten seconds later.

In the fall, I clean and disinfect the camp as carefully as I can. I also wash and dry all the sheets on my bunk and keep them and my sleeping bag in an enclosed plastic container when not in use. Then I declare war on the mice. To keep mice away from me at night, I put out traps in a semicircle around my bunk. Eventually, the survivors catch on and give me plenty of room.

Of course, getting up at night to go outside can be a little dicey with all those traps scattered around, but I keep a pair of slippers in a handy location.

My friend, Jerry, also stays at the camp during deer season; his bunk is just across from mine. He isn't very fond of mice either but considers them more of a nuisance and has adopted a live-and-let-live philosophy.

I stay at the camp all season but Jerry comes and goes. One season, while Jerry was gone, we had a weasel in the camp. Normally, I wouldn't care because weasels catch mice. But because I was staying at the camp, I decided I didn't want to share my sleeping bag with a weasel so I set a large rat trap under Jerry's bunk to try to catch him.

Later that season, after being home for a couple of days, Jerry came back to the camp. The weasel and the rat trap I had set under the edge of his bed had completely slipped my mind.

After happy hour, dinner and a sauna, we turned in. Jerry was just about to jump in his sack when he stepped on the trap. SNAP! It nailed him right across his big toe. He howled bloody murder and started jumping around like a lunatic. I couldn't believe his language. He's normally so mild mannered and easy going; I didn't think he knew those words. I was proud of him; he was human after all. "You idiot!" he screamed. "Look what you've done to my toe! I'll get you for this!"

OUTDOOR FOLLIES

"Me an idiot? You're the one with the broken toe. Why don't you watch where you put your feet? You know I have traps set around here. I've got enough trouble with my own feet much less worrying about yours. Jeez."

"I can survive stepping in a mouse trap," he said, cooling down, "but not a bear trap. Why the heck didn't you tell me it was under my bunk?"

"I forgot."

I planned to sleep with one eye open while Jerry was at the camp but he eventually forgot the incident, or at least I thought he had forgotten it. He stayed overnight and then went home, planning to come back in a couple of days.

When he came back, I still hadn't caught the weasel but I had removed the trap from under his bed and told him so. "Thanks," he snorted derisively, "you probably moved it to my sleeping bag."

"Now there's a thought," I replied.

Later that day, Jerry casually mentioned that he'd seen the weasel that afternoon running across my bunk. That bothered me a little but the weasel had been staying away from my bunk during the night, so I wasn't particularly concerned. I turned in at the usual time and was just about to fall asleep when I heard some noise. "Jerry," I said, "did you
hear that?"

"No, I didn't hear anything," he said. Which didn't surprise me because he's nearly stone deaf.

Eventually I fell asleep. I was just about to pass from a light sleep to a sound sleep, when in a semiconscious state, I felt something on my sleeping bag. It took a second to register but eventually I snapped wide awake! I glanced at Jerry but he was in his bunk and appeared to be sound asleep. I hesitated, and then I felt it again. Something was walking up my sleeping bag toward my head and it wasn't small. I leaped up in a panic, slamming my head on the loft's low ceiling and nearly knocking myself silly. "There's something running on my sleeping bag!" I screamed. Then I heard Jerry snicker. Turning on the light I caught him trying to hide a fishing pole with a fake rat tied to the monofilament line. "You dirty #@%&!" I yelled. "Do you think that's funny? Do you think it would be funny if I threw you down the stairs? I can't believe you'd do such an awful thing just because you were dumb enough to step on a rat trap. I should have put that trap in your sleeping bag. I nearly died of fright, not to mention a possible concussion from hitting the ceiling. I'm gonna get you for this!"

I finally cooled off and forgot about retribution, for the time being anyway. It was time to call a truce and hunt deer.

This wasn't the first time Jerry has played a trick on somebody who was hard at work trying to keep the mice at bay.

A few years earlier, Jerry and I, our friend, Billy C., and his brother-in-law, Jack, were at a fly-in fishing camp in northern Ontario. Billy and Jack got along well except that each thought himself the better trapper.

We soon found that the camp was full of mice. "Not a problem," Billy said, "there are some mouse traps in the kitchen. I'll have these mice trapped out in no time."

"I can set those traps," Jack said. "I've been trapping all my life."

"You've been trapping all your life?" Billy snorted, "you might have set a few traps during your life but I've set thousands! I'll trap these mice."

"By golly, I can catch mice just as well as you! You can have half the traps and I'll take the other half. We'll see who is the better trapper," Jack insisted.

Jerry and I were amused. It's fun to watch grown men argue like two year olds. The opportunity to agitate was more than I could resist. "Why are you setting that trap under the couch? Wouldn't it be better to set it along the wall?" I asked Jack. "Billy told me that mice always run along the wall."

"Ha! What does he know? Sure, if you are not using bait that would be better but if you're using bait, like I am, it's best to have the trap in an area where it can spring without the possible hindrance of a wall. Why would you give me a suggestion from him anyway? I've trapped more mice than he ever has," Jack retorted angrily.

"I don't know," I replied, "It seemed like the thing to do. If it's as easy to trap mice as it is to trap you, we shouldn't have any trouble cleaning the mice out."

Jack looked at me confused, then scowled and went back to setting his traps.

We shut off the light and hit the sack. We weren't in bed more than a few minutes when "snap!" one of the traps went off. Both Billy and Jack jumped from their bunks simultaneously yelling, "I got one!" They flicked on a light and sure enough, there was a mouse in one of Billy's traps. "I was going to set a trap there but he beat me to it," Jack pouted.

We went back to bed and just as I was about to fall asleep, "snap!" another trap went off. Billy and Jack dove from their bunks to check their traps. This time it was Jack who had scored. "Ha!" he snorted, "just as I thought. I knew it wouldn't take me long to catch up."

Back to bed, except this time we couldn't sleep. It was like watching the Super Bowl with the score tied one to one. We waited anxiously but nothing happened. It was dark, still, quiet and time was ticking away. Suddenly Jerry smacked his hands together and yelled, "there's another one."

Billy and Jack fell for it hook, line and sinker. They leaped from their bunks in a mad scramble, each hoping they'd won the mouse war. Flicking on the lights they scurried from trap to trap only to find each trap just as they'd left it. Confused, they looked at each other suspecting subterfuge, then back at the traps. This wasn't making any sense. Finally, in their presence, Jerry smacked his hands again and said, "there's another one," and they figured it out.

Jerry and I had a good laugh and they went back to bed muttering obscenities.

That was the end of my experiences with mice until the following spring.

I live in an apartment on the shore of Lake Superior. It's a nice quiet place because all the residents, except me, are elderly ladies. That particular spring, my neighbor, Eleanor, tapped on my door.

"Pete," she said, "I think I got a mouse in my apartment."

Eleanor is eighty-seven years old. She's a nice lady and a great neighbor. If I can help her out, I'm happy to do it.

"Don't worry about a mouse. He won't eat much."

"I'm serious," she said, "I think there are mice in this apartment. I'm deathly afraid of mice."

I didn't know how to break the news to her but I knew there were mice in the building because I'd seen one scurry across the basement floor early one morning. Our landlord wouldn't be much help. How could he earn a tidy twenty-five percent on his investment and have his building appreciate, while at the same time take a hefty depreciation deduction on his income tax return, if he had to throw money away on mouse traps, or, God forbid, an exterminator.

"I'll tell you what, Eleanor, I'll run down to the store and get a couple of mouse traps. There's only one mouse and it won't take me long to catch him."

"Oh, you don't have to buy traps. I'll gladly buy them if you catch the mouse. I can hardly sleep at night knowing there's one in my apartment."

Eleanor came by later with a mouse trap. It was called a "humane mouse trap." I'd never heard of such a thing. It was a two-inch by four-inch piece of cardboard with some sort of sticky substance on one side. In theory, the mouse would walk on it and get stuck. Then, according to the instructions, you were to don a pair of heavy leather gloves, pick up the cardboard with the mouse attached to it and drop it into a pail. After driving several blocks away, presumably to the home of someone you dislike, you were to pour water on the trap, which would dissolve the glue and free the mouse.

After reading the directions I thought, "What a kind lady, she must not want to kill the mouse."

"Do you want me to catch the mouse with this contraption?" I asked.

"Yes, why not?"

I explained the directions and she said, "Huh? Catch him on glue? Then drive him to a different neighborhood and let him go?

OUTDOOR FOLLIES

This world keeps getting crazier. Why would anybody catch a mouse and let him go? I wouldn't touch anything with a mouse on it, much less drive it around in my car. I didn't realize what kind of trap this was. I hate mice! Would you mind bringing this trap back to the store and exchanging it for a regular mouse trap?"

So much for humanity. "I'd be happy to," I said.

I exchanged the trap and by the next day her mouse problems were over.

A month later I was leaving my apartment when I heard Eleanor whisper, "Pete."

I looked around, because I couldn't tell where her voice was coming from. "Pete," she whispered again, urgently. Then I noticed that her door was open a crack.

"Is that you, Eleanor?" I asked.

"Yes," she whispered. "I can't open the door any wider, there's a bat in the hallway."

I was in the hallway; I didn't see a bat. "Where?" I asked.

"It's on the ceiling. Rosie from upstairs saw it and called me on the phone."

I looked up at the ceiling and sure enough, there was a small bat clinging to it.

"He won't hurt anything, Eleanor. He'll probably sit there all day. Tonight, when it's dark, I'll open the door and he'll fly out."

"I can't wait until tonight. I've got a hair appointment this morning and Rosie's got a doctor's appointment. We need to get out of our apartments and we're afraid to go out with that bat up there.

"I'll tell you what, Eleanor. I'll loan you my twenty-gauge. You can make a run for your car and if he comes after you, shoot him."

"Pete, I'm serious. Can you do something about that bat? I'm afraid of it."

Since I'm also afraid of bats, I was all for letting the bat find his way out the same way he found his way in. I considered using my shotgun but I wasn't certain how the landlord would feel about an eight-inch hole in the ceiling from a number four twenty-gauge shot shell. He could be fussy about such things. I'd have to figure something else out.

"I'll take care of it," I said, "stay in your apartment and I'll let you know when it's safe to come out."

Actually, I didn't want to mess with the bat either. I mean, when you think about it, they're nothing more than a mouse with wings . . . except perhaps a bit more ornery when aroused. Regardless, my manhood was at stake. I'd have to figure something out.

Our apartment is two stories high and the bat was on the ceiling of the second story of the stairwell. I thought perhaps I could knock him off the ceiling with a broom and he'd fly out the door but I doubted it because the door was about twelve feet below him. I walked up the stairs to the second floor but I still couldn't get at him. I might have been able to knock him down but I wanted to get a good swat at him with a broom and it was too awkward to swing from where I was standing.

After thinking it over, I came up with a plan. I got a large step-ladder from the basement and placed it on the ground floor landing. Then I taped my trout fishing net to the end of an eight-foot drapery rod. The net was fine woven nylon. If I could reach the bat from the top of the stepladder, it would be a cinch to tangle the bat in the net. There was some risk. I might anger the bat while I was standing on the top of the ladder and have it come after me but I'd have to take the chance.

I climbed to the top of the ladder, put the net over the bat and within seconds it was tangled. It was a piece of cake. Climbing down, I felt pretty smug. You gotta get up pretty early in the morning to fool old Pete.

I took the bat out to the parking lot where I tried to shake him out of the net. Nothing doing. He was stuck by one wing and had his teeth clamped down on the netting. He was also becoming increasingly unhappy. Did you know that bats have very large teeth and hiss when they're angry? That got my attention. The more I shook him, the angrier he became. It looked like the only way I could free him was to use my hands and I'll guarantee you, that wasn't going to happen. Also, he was so agitated, I worried that if he did get free he might come for me. I put the net down, walked back into the apartment, got a broom and a couple of whacks later, the bat was finished.

Even after his demise, he was still stuck in the net. I didn't want to touch him so I took a shovel and held the frame of the net to the ground, while at the same time, tried to free the bat by pulling on his wing with a pair of needle-nose pliers. The net was very elastic. The harder I pulled, the more it stretched, until it was as taught as a drawn slingshot. Suddenly, he came free of the netting. I was so surprised that I momentarily relaxed my grip on his wing and he came for me like a heat seeking missile. He nailed me right between the eyes. Good thing I had my mouth closed, I might have eaten the darn thing. I nearly died. It had gotten me in the end.

I ran into the apartment and looked in the mirror and sure enough, there was blood on my forehead. I feared I had been bitten by a dead bat. I ran water in the basin and rinsed my head and looked in the mirror again, imagining all sorts of diseases I might contract from a bat bite but luckily, my skin wasn't broken; the blood I saw had been the bat's.

After cleaning up the mess I knocked on Eleanor's door to let her know it was safe to come out.

"Did you have any trouble?" she asked.

"Trouble? From an itsy-bitsy bat? You can't be serious. No, nothing to it. Feel free to call me anytime you have a problem."

That was a year ago. We made it through last deer season without any major mouse problems, although the mice might not agree since their numbers dropped to a trickle by the end of the season. There is the matter of seeking revenge on Jerry for the nasty trick he played on me. Perhaps a letter from the IRS is in order, something about an audit for the last three years he was in business. I'll have to think about that one . . .

To order a copy of this book.

Web orders: petecrowley.com

Postal orders: Pete Crowley, 65464 Lake Park Road, Ashland, Wisconsin 54806. Please enclose $15.00 plus $5.00 for shipping and handling.

*Wisconsin residents please add $0.83 Wisconsin sales tax.